Casino Chiseler

Leopold Borstinski

NOVEMBER 1950

1

BLINK AND YOU missed it. Alex Cohen's life had flashed past him from the moment he took the bus to Rikers back in '36 and today. This would be his first time in front of the television cameras and an audience of millions.

He ate breakfast in his hotel restaurant—since coming out of jail, he had learned the value of a hearty start to the day because you never knew what your next meal would be. So a plate crammed with fruit, cheese blintzes, and a bagel, washed down with orange juice and coffee. Always with the black coffee. During the feast, Alex read the local paper—a habit he'd picked up from his teenage years in the old country. When he put the newspaper down, he smiled at his lawyer, Mendy Greenberg, who had been waiting all this time.

"Thanks for coming over and helping me with the hearing."

"My pleasure, Alex. It's been a while since I've seen you."

"My parole review. Before the war."

"A lifetime ago."

"Sure feels that way to me. Any last-minute advice?"

"The good news is that you are not on trial this time. But the same rules apply. Don't respond to anything anyone asks you without checking with me first. And do not rise to their bait. Kefauver's desperate to get a head on a spike."

"Just like old times. Different cops, but the same story."

"Remember that Kefauver is worse than a cop—word on the streets of Washington is that he'll stand for election soon."

Alex eyed Mendy, judging his words and considering his response, but before he could speak, he saw that his car had appeared and was ready out front.

As they headed over to the courthouse, he continued their breakfast conversation.

"One thing you never explained to me was why I only got five years."

"What do you mean?"

"You were expecting them to throw the book at me, but I was inside for three years, tops."

"Not everyone walked away from you back then. While nobody could be seen to support you, efforts were being made to ease your burden."

"Who?"

"Here we are. Don't speak a word to the press hounds. Do as I say and you will get through this just fine."

The car pulled over and Mendy leaped straight out, followed by Alex.

BULBS POPPED AND whizzed about his head as the crime reporters swarmed around him, hoping to catch the best photo of Alex for their front-page noon editions. Local cops lined his route from the curbside to the court entrance. Perhaps for the first time in his life, he was grateful to a bunch of flatfeet.

The crowd thickened at the bottom of the courthouse steps, forcing Mendy and Alex to pause their attempts to proceed.

"What you going to tell Kefauver?"

"Are you naming any names today?"

"How does it feel to be back in court?"

A thousand questions whirred around his ears as each reporter did their best to get a quote for their editor, but Alex followed Mendy's instructions and said nothing.

A handful of reporters stayed with them as they entered the hallowed portals of the courthouse building, and Mendy asked a nearby court official where they needed to go. The answer delivered them to a wide corridor packed with men and women standing around, looking like they had as much idea of what was going on as Alex did.

"Brace yourself, the world and his wife are watching us."

Into the courtroom and an usher showed them to the front right-hand benches. Alex surveyed the joint: an arc of seats, for the senators to question their witnesses, sat opposite with a bank of tables and chairs for them and their lawyers. Behind, the auditorium was packed with a mixture of concerned citizens, members of the press, and court ghouls who'd turn up to the opening of a paper bag if it took place in this building.

To the wings, either side of the tables in front of the politicians' pews, were enormous boxes on wheels—the television cameras. Alex swallowed hard. Mendy nudged him and leaned in.

"Don't worry about the TV crew. They are not your enemy—the senators are the ones who'll question you. Everything else is fluff. Stick to the script and if you think you will deviate from the plan, then stop and speak with me."

A HUSH FELL over the room and Alex twisted round to see what was happening. If he had remained facing forward, he would have seen a side door open and a stream of senators gush into the courtroom and take their seats in the arc in front of him. No sooner had they appeared than the lights on top of the television cameras glowed red, showing they were live on air across the country.

After an interminable wait for everyone to sit down, open their cases, shuffle their papers, and settle into their seats, the first witness was called. Alex strode over to the center of the tables with Mendy by his side.

A court official stepped forward and asked Alex to swear to tell the truth, the whole truth, and pretty much only the truth before his God. When this activity started, the TV cameras swung around and focused their rays on him. Despite being unsettled by this mechanical response, Alex sat down, leaning forward so that his elbows rested on the table and he interleaved the fingers of one hand in between those of the other. Then he exhaled and stared forward at the cockroach in front of him, Estes Kefauver.

"Let's keep this simple, shall we, gentlemen?"

Those beady eyes bore inside him and Alex swallowed hard again.

"Mr. Cohen, let me remind you that you are under oath. Are you, or have you ever been, an active participant in the organized crime syndicate known as the mafia?"

November 1941

2

ALEX'S PLAN FROM the moment he arrived in Sing Sing was to get out of there as quickly as possible. He listened to his lawyer's advice and they devised a two-prong strategy. Mendy appealed the sentence and Alex kept his nose clean and behaved like a model prisoner.

The first few months were the worst, in no small measure because he had hope to cling to—every time he saw him, Mendy talked about how he had found another line of argument, a different way to pursue Alex's freedom. By January, Alex realized this would not happen and instructed his lawyer to stop trying on his behalf—Alex was spending his hidden fixed income on legal fees with nothing to show for it.

Instead, he followed the guards' instructions to the letter. Never groused and always kept out of everybody else's business. In prison, that is not easy if you have a reputation like Alex's. Most of the cons believed he would sprinkle pixie dust over their circumstances, bribe a judge and get them out. As Alex explained repeatedly, if that was within his power then he would have done it for himself.

To pretend that he experienced ordinary prison time would be an exaggeration. Sure, he was locked in his cell and forced to do the bidding of the guards, but they also knew that he was connected to the most powerful criminals in the history of America and Alex let them hold that belief, even though those self-same syndicate members had left him beached, isolated, and with no support.

The other element that made his jail time more pleasant was his gelt. Alex had gifted two-thirds of his wealth to his ex-wife Sarah and their sons and had hidden his last million before he entered the portals of Sing Sing. That still left him with a small fortune to rely on in prison and grease any palms that needed it.

WHEN ALEX WALKED out of Sing Sing, nobody was waiting to meet him and he took a bus back to New York. This was a simple message from the syndicate that his time with them was over—his friends had turned their backs on him before his trial even began, and he'd expected no less upon his return to the outside world.

Still, there was a sinking feeling in the pit of his stomach as he realized he was on his own again. He considered looking up his old lieutenants, Ezra and Massimo, but thought better of it. Time had passed and they were best shot of him. Just like his family—Sarah hadn't visited him once, nor had he seen his boys since before the trial began. He was alone.

The smartest thing to do next was to leave town and head west, away from the sphere of influence of Charlie Luciano, Meyer Lansky, and Benny Siegel, as well as other members of the inner circle of organized crime like Albert Anastasia and Louis Buchalter.

While Chicago was an obvious destination, there were too many tentacles reaching out from the Eastern Seaboard into the Windy City so Alex chose Los Angeles as a fresh base from which to operate.

These thoughts permeated his mind as, years later, he sat on a train from LA to Detroit—he had a contract to fulfill in the city his old friend Abe Bernstein had called home. It was a lifetime since they'd spoken and, besides, the purpose of his visit had nothing to do with the leader of the Sugar Hill Gang and everything to do with a lowlife piece of trash known as Jem Cole.

WITH JUST AN address written on a piece of paper and the memory of the instructions issued to him by Jack Dragna back on the west coast, he found a fleapit hotel to rest overnight before doing the job the following day.

"The scumbag has shown me nothing but disrespect, Alex."

"I understand, Jack. Do you want him to suffer before he meets his end?"

"An apology would be nice, but don't sweat it. Just make sure he's deceased before you leave him."

From what Alex could figure, Jem Cole had taken a fancy to one of Jack's mistresses and had made the foolish mistake of being seen in a restaurant on Sunset Boulevard with her. Gili Earl was innocent in that she knew she shouldn't have agreed to the date, but she argued that it was only a bite to eat, whereas the kid had no such excuse. There was no way he only wanted to break bread with the long-legged brunette. So Gili's punishment was to no longer be Jack's skirt, and Alex was dispatched to Detroit in search of the guy.

He wasn't hard to find the following day because Jack had sent the boy on a fool's errand to isolate him from his crew—there was no need to put Alex in harm's way, and Jack reckoned Alex deserved a brief vacation, anyway.

The address Jack gave Alex was a residential building in the heart of the city and a quick check with the janitor confirmed the guy was in. At the top of the two flights of stairs, Alex pressed his ear to the apartment door to see if he could hear anyone inside. Nothing. So he rang the doorbell and waited.

After thirty long seconds, there was no response and Alex tried the bell again. Another wait and still nobody. He sighed—he surely didn't have the patience for this anymore and just wanted the job to be over with. Was he getting too old for bursting into people's apartments and shooting them in cold blood? Now was an opportunity to find out.

One swift kick and the door flew inward and landed on the hallway floor. Nobody stirred, and he considered the possibility that the concierge had got it wrong. He looked down at the number on the door and checked he had the right apartment.

Pulling out his revolver, Alex strode into the living room and found no one. Then he marched into what appeared to be a bedroom and discovered Jem, face down on the bed with several liquor bottles on the floor. The guy was out cold and Alex hoped it was only the booze and not that someone had got to the kid first. If somebody had made the hit before him, then he couldn't collect his fee in good conscience.

He bent down and smelled the whiskey on Jem's breath—just at the point when an enormous snore erupted out of his mouth, spewing a burst of air into Alex's face. He stood up straight and slapped the guy on the thigh with the side of his pistol.

A trip to the bathroom and Alex poured a glass of cold water on the fella's head and, amid much spluttering and swearing, Jem roused himself from his deep alcohol-fueled slumber.

"What the f—"

"Save it, Jem."

The barrel of Alex's gun was aimed right in the center of Jem's torso and the guy had sufficient presence of mind to remain still, and he eased back down on his bed, head resting on his pillow.

"Who are you?"

"It doesn't matter who I am. Instead, you should ask me why I am here."

Alex allowed Jem a few seconds to contemplate his suggestion, but as nothing was forthcoming, Alex continued the one-sided conversation.

"Last week you were seen out with Gili Earl. Do you remember that night?"

A nod confirmed Cole's memory.

"Did you have a great time?"

"Yeah…"

"Do you think Gili enjoyed herself?"

"Reckon so. There were no complaints."

"Was the food satisfactory?"

"Sure thing. I have never tasted such a great ribeye in my life."

"Wow. And how'd you fair later in the evening?"

"A fella don't like to brag."

"How very gallant. Did you get to first base?"

"Home run, my friend."

Cole winked at Alex as though they were compadres—for a moment, he forgot the situation he was in.

"Congratulations. Sounds as though you had a fabulous night all round—wonderful food, fantastic company, great lay. Things couldn't have worked out better, right?"

"I reckon."

"Wrong, Jem. Remember I asked you to think about why I'm here? Any ideas?"

Cole shook his head. This was all too confusing before his first smoke of the day. His eyes darted left and right until Alex offered him a cigarette, which he took, lighting it himself with a book of matches on his nightstand table.

"You made a mistake and I am here to correct that error."

"What was that? The skirt wasn't complaining when I left her, if you see what I mean?"

"Sure do, Jem, but that's not what I'm talking about. Did you know who Gili was before you took her for the meal?"

"One of the local girls. Why does it matter, and what are you doing hounding me in Detroit of all places?"

"She wasn't just any girl—she was Jack Dragna's skirt."

Alex allowed that idea to float in the air and mingle with the cigarette smoke being exhaled by Jem. The guy's expression shifted from youthful arrogance over his sexual conquest to wide-eyed fear at the implication that he'd messed around with a Dragna moll.

"I didn't know, mister. You gotta believe me."

"What I think about what you did is irrelevant—I'm just a hired hand. Are you sorry for what you have done?"

"Of course, Mac. If I had known, then I wouldn't have touched that ass with a six-foot pole."

"I guess that counts as an apology, doesn't it?"

"Certainly does, mister."

Alex inhaled, fired three shots into Jem's chest, and when the body stopped twitching half a minute later, he squeezed another shot into the guy's face at close range. Then he popped into the bathroom to make sure there were no blood spatters and left the apartment. He considered propping up the front door, still lying on the ground, but it wasn't worth the effort. Down the two flights and out onto the street. Jem Cole wouldn't be ruining any more of Jack's women.

3

AS ALEX ARRIVED at the station, he looked up at the information board and spotted Hoboken as one of the many possible destinations from Detroit. The sound of his sons' laughter filled his head and he changed his plans—he'd visit them there instead of heading straight back to LA.

He dropped a dime to Jack to confirm that the contract had been carried out and then made a second call to Sarah to make sure he would be welcome when he showed up. The train was worth waiting two hours for if he had a chance of seeing his boys.

When he arrived in New Jersey, he hopped a cab and checked into a hotel near to Sarah's home, which he'd bought for her a decade before. Although she and her lawyer friend had moved in together before Alex did time, she had insisted Kameron Jacobs sold his place and she kept hold of her house.

He hung up his clothes in his room, dialed out, and, to his surprise, Sarah answered.

"Hi there. How are things?"

"All good. You?"

"Fine, thanks. I've just got in and have arrived at my hotel."

"Which one?"

"The Radcliffe, which isn't that far from your place."

"When were you wanting to come over?"

"I was hoping for tonight but I understand that's very short notice."

"And some. Why not pop round tomorrow at three?"

"Will Kameron be there?"

"No, Alex. He and I aren't together any more."

Alex was surprised—he'd figured they'd be an item for quite some time. The guy was a stand-up fella who brought in the money and made few demands on Sarah, from what little she had said on their rare phone calls.

"Since when?"

"A while. Let's sort out the details about tomorrow and you can cross-examine me when you come over."

THE NEXT AFTERNOON, Alex arrived on time, sauntered up the path to the front door, and rang the bell. A young woman answered and let him in—he assumed she was the housekeeper, judging by how she behaved as he smiled on the porch.

He stood in the living room and edged toward the rear of the house where the sounds of youthful exuberance were bubbling away. Through the kitchen and out into the backyard until he bumped into the three youngest messing about with a football. Moishe and David, his eldest, were nowhere to be found.

"They'll be home later—they are at work."

Sarah's voice startled him for a second, but the calm tones set Alex at ease almost immediately.

"Living the other side of the country, it's hard to remember those two are old enough to earn gelt."

"Moishe insists on paying for his keep and won't take a single penny from me."

"We both know that's because he believes your money comes from a poisoned well."

"That has never been how I have described your generosity toward us, Alex."

"I understand that, but it is the way the boy thinks."

"The man is stubborn in his beliefs. Any idea where he might have got that trait?"

At that point, Arik spotted his papa and rushed over, forgetting himself for a minute. Then he checked himself the final fifteen feet and brought himself down to a slow saunter. His disappearance from the football field meant the game was over and the other two followed him in.

"Hey, Papa. What brings you to New Jersey?"

"To visit you fellas, of course."

"Yeah, right. I thought you were living in California."

"Don't ask your father about his business. Be glad he is here to see us. The man has traveled six thousand miles and you're giving him an inquisition."

"Aw, I was only pulling your leg, Papa."

Arik leaped forward and gave his father an enormous hug. As the youngest of the clan, the boy had yet to shed all his childish ways or be so concerned about how the others perceived him.

Asher and Elijah were a year or two older and were more cautious in their dealings with their father. Perhaps because their recollections were stronger of the shouting between their parents—or they had deeper memories of the night when their bedroom was strafed with bullets. Either way, they tolerated this man in their midst but didn't want to show much enthusiasm for Alex's existence. And even though it hurt him, he understood why.

They hung in the garden for the next three hours. The boys let Alex play in their ball games; other times he'd sit on the grass and take pleasure in watching them have fun near him. All the while, Sarah tried to remain indoors. True to her word when they got divorced, she always wanted to give Alex the best opportunities available to spend time with his sons.

SHE INVITED HIM to stay for dinner and he accepted—he enjoyed being surrounded by these people, his family. Holding guest status meant Sarah forced him to sit down in the living room while the boys laid the table and helped in the kitchen; their mama had them well trained.

She offered him a drink, but he declined and sat back, letting the domesticity engulf him. When was the last time he'd been in an ordinary house doing normal things? He had missed out on this by not being at home when he and Sarah were together and then being away after they split up.

David arrived back first and strode toward his father with arms outstretched.

"Good to see you, Pop."

"You're looking in excellent form, son."

"Can't complain, you know how it is."

Just before David embellished on his initial thoughts, Moishe's key jangled in the lock and David stood transfixed, aware of his elder brother's feelings about their father.

Moishe took one look at his old man and walked straight up the stairs, a blink of the eyes his only recognition that Alex was in the building. Alex sighed but had expected nothing less. David fake-punched him on the shoulder.

"Don't worry about him. He's just got some more growing up to do, Pop."

"He is living his life by his own set of rules. I can't fault him for that."

MOISHE WAS THE last to sit at the dinner table, but Sarah made everyone wait until he arrived before they started. She didn't admonish the man in front of the others, but she had followed him upstairs when he first got home. He was a man and needed to be treated accordingly.

"This is a fine meal, thank you, Sarah."

"You should have been here last chweek. The turkey was the size of a Buick."

Moishe shot daggers at Arik—the eldest son failed to understand why the youngest was prepared to even talk to their father. After all, Arik was the one who had been kidnapped at gunpoint—Moishe saw no reason to forgive the man for that traumatic afternoon in their lives.

"Last week?" What was so special about a meal several days before? Then Alex's eyes widened: Thanksgiving, a celebration he had never seen the point in. Takings were always down because every joe citizen stayed at home in the bosom of his family and, when he ran speakeasies and cathouses throughout Manhattan, Alex regretted that they didn't want to spend their free time in the bosoms of his *nafkas*. He smiled at his own joke.

"What's funny?" asked Elijah.

"Nothing much. Just happy to be here."

"Shame you didn't bother trying to be with us all the previous days of our lives."

"Moishe!"

"That's all right, Sarah. While his tone was disrespectful, Moishe is correct. I should have spent more time with you guys—especially when we were married."

"Cheap words, old man."

Alex's eldest son stood up and stormed out of the room.

"I am so sorry, Alex."

"Don't be, Sarah—you shouldn't apologize on his behalf. Moishe's a man nowadays and he must behave like one. And seek forgiveness like one when he needs to."

LATER ON, AFTER they tucked the kids up in bed, the adults remained and then David took his leave so that Alex and Sarah were alone.

"I find it hard to imagine he's working to be a lawyer some day."

"I know, Alex. It is hard to believe that any of them will do anything apart from play ball in the backyard."

"There is that. How's Moishe doing? Accountant, right?"

"Yes. It's taking him longer than David because he refuses to take a dime from me, like I was saying earlier."

"He's a fool to be so stubborn, but you have to hand it to him."

"I know. He can be annoyingly righteous."

Alex chuckled.

"The apple doesn't fall far from the tree, does it, Sarah?"

She grinned back and took a swig of her drink—a large Scotch on the rocks.

"How are you, Sarah? I'm sorry, but I had no idea that Kameron was out of the picture."

"Why would you? Since you moved to the west coast, we've hardly spoken."

"And before that, I was inside and my phone calls were limited… Who ended it, you or him?"

"Me. After a year, we had settled into a rut and I couldn't see we were going anywhere. He was a reasonable provider—not as good as you, naturally—but he was in the room yet not there for me. Kameron was the kind of guy who would always be more interested in listening to a match on the radio than talking to his wife. And now I'm alone."

"Has there been anybody since then?"

"No. I can't face putting myself through the dating scene and Hoboken isn't as metropolitan as Manhattan so people still stare at me, because they notice I have no man and look after all these kids. Some who don't know me very well assume I lost my husband in the war. Those who I have allowed into my life have some understanding of what it must be like for me to be your ex-wife."

"We could always get together again if you want," Alex chuckled, not knowing whether he was joking.

"I'll get back to you on that."

4

BACK AT HIS apartment in Boyle Heights in the heart of the most Jewish area of Los Angeles, Alex sat in an easy chair enjoying his newspaper after another heavy breakfast. He did the washing up and then sat back into the cushioning and flipped from page to page.

Just before he reached the sports section, there was a knock on his door. With nobody expected, Alex was cautious as he approached the entrance and squinted through the fish-eye before he relaxed.

"Come in. You were the last person I'd have thought would darken this cave."

Meyer Lansky walked in and took off his hat before carrying on into the living room, and settling into the couch. This middle-aged Jew was more than a guy from his past—he was the syndicate's financier and had been one of Alex's closest business partners before his incarceration, going all the way back to the start of Prohibition.

"Coffee?"

"Yes, please, and some cheesecake if you have it."

"You must be confused—this isn't Lindy's."

They both smiled and Alex popped into the kitchen to prepare their drinks. When he came back, Meyer had spread out on the couch and sat like he owned the place. Alex passed him his mug and returned to his easy chair.

"I almost drove past your block, Alex. I thought you'd have been in a different part of town."

"Richer, you mean."

"Well, I wouldn't have put it quite that way."

"I would. We used to say we live together, we love together but the minute Dewey came after me and threw me in jail, you all turned your backs on me. This isn't a complaint and I am thrilled to see you today, but there is a reason I'm no longer in clover."

Meyer sipped his coffee as he listened to his erstwhile friend.

"Remember, at that time, we were all nervous about how far the special prosecutor would go to nail all of us. People closed ranks, but it was always business and nothing personal."

"I understand. I'm hoping you can tell from my tone that while I was not happy about the situation, I do not bear any ill will—to you, Charlie, or Benny."

"We all did what we had to do—or could do."

Meyer's last statement made little sense, but Alex let it go. The truth was that he was horrified over the speed with which his friends had walked away from him when he needed help most.

"And I've been doing my best since I got out of jail too."

"How are things going for you?"

"I get by, Meyer. I've been careful to file my taxes each year and to make sure that Uncle Sam didn't shine a flashlight into my more private investments. So I don't flaunt my money, but I am doing all right."

"When I arrived at this building, I was concerned for you."

"This is a friendly neighborhood—there might be nothing as fine as Lindy's but I can buy bagels and cheesecake from the local stores."

"I'm glad you are making your way."

"I said I get by—and nothing more. You know that I work for Jack Dragna now."

"Why yes, he's mentioned it to me."

"Did he ask for a reference?"

Alex smiled and Meyer returned the favor.

"Let's just say he asked my opinion of you as a contract killer."

"Thank you for the kind word because he has kept me busy since I landed on this side of the country."

"*Gornisht*. It was the least I could do, and besides, you are a terrific marksman. Those years in France weren't wasted on you."

The weeks he'd spent cowering in fox holes in French and Belgian fields and the fact they had given him a Purple Heart for killing a kid in the middle of the war. Nothing made sense then, and not much more did now.

"And how is the old gang?"

"Charlie remains behind bars and Mendy has stopped trying to get him released. They gave him thirty years and it looks like he'll serve every one of them."

"Dutch Schultz was right—we should have killed Dewey while we had the chance."

"You reckon? Murdering the special prosecutor would not have stopped Charlie's trial. Now you are agreeing with Anastasia—he was hot for bumping off the cop back then, and I never thought I'd see the day when you two agreed on anything."

"Him and Buchalter. They still rule the roost in Brownsville?"

"Lepke went on the lam and then was arrested two years ago. You'll love this—they indicted him for the Joe Rosen murder and we hear the decision next week."

"I can't pretend to be sad that Lepke is in trouble. What about Anastasia?"

"He is still a syndicate member, although he has offered a six-figure reward to get rid of a little local difficulty he's facing."

"I wondered when you'd cut to the chase and tell me why you came all this way to make a house call."

"Alex, I have a proposition for you and it is worth one hundred thousand dollars."

"FOR THAT KIND of money, you have got my attention, Meyer."

"I thought I might. This is a hit like almost no other, which is why we wanted to go to someone we could count on to get it done, despite its challenges."

"You've stroked my ego, now tell me who are the people who trust me sufficiently to kill someone, but not enough to be invited back to the top table of the syndicate."

"Alex, I want you to listen to me and believe every word I say. The old guard know and respect you and almost all would like to see your return, but the newer members are nervous about accepting you into the fold since your time in jail. They hold a belief that your short prison sentence came at a price. Their words, not mine."

"I kept *schtum*. Dewey got nothing from me, other prisoners got nothing from me, and the governor of Sing Sing got nothing either."

"Don't shoot the messenger, Alex. You asked a question and I am giving you the answer you deserve."

"Yet they still want my help."

"The hit we have in mind is far from easy to achieve, and if it is timed well, it will be significant for the syndicate."

"Go on."

Alex wasn't so much sulking as deeply unhappy with the situation. For Meyer to assert the syndicate couldn't trust him was an insult. Under any other circumstance, or if he was any other person, the fella would be dead by now, but the two men had enough shared history—and personal respect—that Alex allowed the man the opportunity to pitch him a hit of a lifetime.

"An individual has named Louis and Albert as leaders of Murder Corporation and for being responsible for a string of murders. Their accuser is about to testify against them, and we wish this person to breathe no more."

"Let me get this straight, you want me to save Buchalter and Anastasia. The two guys who stole the heroin business from under me and Charlie?"

"Let's not rake over those coals again, Alex. If the hit happens before Louis' latest trial then he will be spared the chair. And Albert won't even get charged."

"This gets better by the minute. You want me to save the pair of them."

"Yes, Alex."

He was silent for a spell, mulling over the implications of Meyer's words. There had been a lot of time since he last saw his fellow directors of Murder Corporation, and the irony wasn't lost on him that he was being dragged back to New York to save their sorry asses. Given the number of killers in Brownsville, couldn't the syndicate have found somebody closer? The importance of the hit had driven Meyer to California and into Alex's home, but it didn't sit well with him.

"Who's the mark?"

"Abe Reles—he heard Louis issue the order for the contract on the trucker, Joe Rosen."

Alex was less than a week away from the start of his trial, and Rosen was the last contract he did for the Murder Corporation before being forced to step down by Anastasia and Buchalter. Funny how the syndicate's single biggest supplier of assassins for hire was the man to turn state's evidence. He'd always liked Reles—the guy had a simplicity to the way he behaved and no matter what the time of day or the distance that needed to be traveled, Abe could be relied on to know somebody who could down tools and perform a hit on the spin of a nickel.

"Where is the stool pigeon holed up?"

"He's in a hotel in New York. Before you agree to the job, you should understand that he is being guarded all day and night by cops. They will shoot you on sight to protect their star witness."

"Would a sniper rifle not be easier than walking into the place?"

"We've had a guy staring at the window through a scope for three days now, but Abe hasn't been seen at all. The police are smarter than they used to be, Alex, and this must appear to be an accident. There cannot be even a hint of foul play."

"If I do this, will I get back into the syndicate?"

"I can't promise that, Alex. It can only help your case but don't bank on it. The money is the payment and nothing more."

"Two hundred thousand, did you say?"

"No, I said half that."

"If you want me to save Anastasia's life, the cost goes up."

"But, Alex, if you hope to return to the syndicate then the price must remain the same. It is a generous amount by anybody's standards."

He stood up and walked over to Meyer to shake his hand and seal the deal. Lansky gave him the details of the hotel and an envelope with some spending money.

"After the job, you should visit Cuba—there are plenty of opportunities for a man like you and the lifestyle is so less squalid than the City of Angels. And if that's too big a trip for you, then swing by Benny Siegel. He's in Las Vegas nowadays and would be happy to work with a reliable fella like yourself from the good old days."

5

ALEX TOOK THE train to New York, his first time back since the day he got out of Sing Sing and passed through when he'd spent three hours in the station before heading west. He was too embarrassed to even try a visit to his boys in Hoboken.

With an overnight stopover in Chicago, the journey only took two days before he reached Penn and went about finding a bed for the night. The streets were all in the same place, but everything was different. Maybe it was the fact he was forced to stay off Times Square instead of a more upmarket location. Perhaps Alex was just completely alone—an experience he had not felt in Manhattan since the day his family arrived from the old country.

No expense was spared at the fleapit known as the Hotel Bristol on Thirty-Ninth and Sixth. In fact, no expense was spent either. The joint hadn't seen a lick of paint since the Great War, and the receptionist might have been witness to the birth of the nation.

Alex did his best to ignore the peeling wallpaper and acrid stench in the corridors. Instead, he threw his clothes in the wardrobe and hit the street to grab a bite to eat in a nearby diner before keeping his head down and taking every precaution not to be recognized—now or after the job.

The next day, he took a train and ferry out to Coney Island. As the vessel chugged its way along the Hudson, Alex's mind cast back to the time he and his teenage girlfriend, Rebecca, had made the same journey. He had won her a toy at the fair and they had got stuck at the top of a Ferris wheel. When the boat docked, the enormous ride still turned slowly and a bitter smile ripped across Alex's face. That afternoon had been one of the happiest of his life, but now this place meant nothing to him.

Two blocks away from the main thoroughfare was the Half Moon Hotel. The frontage comprised a brick wall and a crescent-shaped sign above the unassuming entranceway. There were four vehicles in the parking lot, all black saloons—reeking of cop.

Alex scouted around the perimeter of the Half Moon and found the hotel was split into two sections. The main building comprised ten stories and a second was attached to it, only four stories high. The rear hotel rooms overlooked the lower effort, but all he had was a room number and the sight of a plainclothes detective leaning against the back wall beside each of the two staff entrances.

Before he could hatch a plan, Alex needed to look inside, but achieving even that goal would not be simple. And he couldn't be sure having entered the joint that he could perform the same feat twice and not be spotted.

The only option was to wing it and wait for nightfall before taking the risk of breaking and entering. Also, he needed to go one block west to make sure the getaway vehicle was positioned where Meyer had promised it. Without that, he would have to stick around for the ferry to set sail and that was no way to leave the scene of a crime.

HAVING WALKED TO the car and chugged down a burger and fries along with a cup of coffee, Alex waited until darkness fell in a local bar. Old habits died hard because he spent the entire evening hugging a single beer at the back of the establishment, hiding in the shadows.

By eleven, he thought he had given more than enough time for Abe Reles to get to bed. Tomorrow was his day to shine in court, so the officers on his protection detail would have insisted he had an early night. Even if they hadn't, Alex's impatience got the better of him, so he threw two bucks down for a tip and headed out into the evening air.

A circuitous trip around Coney Island brought Alex back to the Half Moon. His natural professional caution prevented him from taking a direct route. Anyone seeing this gray figure in a fedora wouldn't think twice about him and would be hard-pushed to notice him heading toward his intended destination.

At the rear of the hotel, the two flatfeet remained glued to the walls, so that didn't look a promising start. Alex wandered round to the front and hung back at the far side of the parking lot, squatting between a low wall and a car that had arrived since his last sortie. A silence descended on the area, punctuated by the occasional distant whoop from the fair.

His patience paid dividends because fifteen long minutes later, a group of men and women appeared and made their way to the entrance. They were chatting to each other and, with so many people swirling around, nobody noticed Alex tag along at the back and join them as the party entered the hotel and lined up at the reception desk to get their keys.

Before they had a chance to disperse, he slipped to one side and made straight for the stairwell. Even though there was a cop sat in the lobby, there were too many moving bodies for the guy to see Alex peel off, let alone glimpse his face.

Up four flights of stairs and he hugged the wall next to the solid wooden doorway. He pressed his ear to the surface–nothing. First, he placed his hand on the handle, and then he turned it ever so slowly, waiting for the inevitable sight of another gumshoe on the other side.

With the door open ten inches, Alex popped his head into the residential space–two corridors met in an L-shape at the stairwell. Sensible location for a fire escape. Along the left were double doors fifty feet away and to the right was nothing but a long corridor filled with nothing but a pair of shoes at the far end, resting in the inky darkness.

Alex edged toward the double doors and monitored the room numbers—517, 519, 521… then the doors. One thing was sure: his quarry in 523 was on the other side and, therefore, there would be at least a patrolman from the protection detail five feet in front—unseen right now but present, nonetheless. He inhaled, felt for the piece in his pants, and pushed the door open.

A chair met him with no guard. Strange, but Alex was happy to take the good fortune. Keeping his hand on his revolver, he opened the door and, as casually as a hitman can, walked into Abe Reles' hotel room.

RELES WAS ASLEEP, sat up in his bed, clothed with a book on his lap. When Alex closed the door behind himself, Abe woke up with a start and his jaw dropped when he recognized his guest.

"What the…"

"Save it, Abe."

Alex pulled his gun and kept it aimed at Reles, while he circled around the room to make the guy's torso an easier target. Reles never took his eyes off him during this maneuver, even when he sidled over to the adjoining door and checked that the en suite was empty.

"Nice place you got here, Abe."

"They're looking after me just swell."

"The cops want something from you, that's why. It's not because of your charismatic charm."

"I know. You do what you gotta do."

"That may well be the difference between you and me, Abe. See, back in the day, I was up against that special prosecutor Dewey and he gave me the option to sing like a canary. I refused."

He shot daggers into Reles' eyes, a mix of deep disgust and sheer hatred.

"Look where it got you, though, Alex. The cops sent you up the river, and from what I heard, the syndicate turned their back on you. How long were you in jail?"

"Five-year sentence but out with good behavior."

Reles laughed—his book fell off his lap and landed with a thud on the floor.

"Good behavior? How much did you have to suck in to survive? And I'm not in your league—never have been."

"Abe, it is not a competition, but there are some things you just shouldn't do."

"In case you haven't noticed, we're not Sicilian. We are Jewish and the vow of omertà doesn't apply to us."

"It's the same code of silence, whoever you are. What the hell drove you to squeal, anyway?"

"Louis and Anastasia screwed me. Then they put a hit on me. I was trapped in a corner when the Feds offered me a way out. If I hadn't taken their deal, we wouldn't be talking right now."

His voice trailed off as he pondered what Alex was doing in his room—other than passing the time of day.

"I didn't trust Louis or Albert either—they stole from me too, but when I had the opportunity, there was no way I could squeal."

"You'd have done the same if you were in my shoes, Alex. It's easy to make pronouncements when there isn't a contract out on your head."

"That may be so, Abe, but I never squealed. Besides, what do you think will happen to you for the rest of your life? Are the Feds going to guard you day and night?"

"They've got plans to keep me safe—you don't have to worry about that… Hey, how did you get in here? Wasn't there a detective outside my door?"

Alex shook his head. Abe's question was a good one. The chances of the flatfoot taking a leak during his shift were close to zero. If Meyer could organize a getaway vehicle, then perhaps he could orchestrate other things too.

"No one was there to protect you, Abe. I walked straight in here. Nobody stopped or frisked me. Up the stairs and here I am."

Reles gulped and his fingers gripped the blankets at the implication of his guards' absence. Alex sighed and glanced out of the window. The room was at the rear of the hotel, on the side that overlooked the second, lower building.

"I need you to stand up, Abe."

"You don't have to do this, Alex."

"We both know that's not true. I might have been somebody in the syndicate when we last met, but now I'm just a hired gun. Get up."

The final two words were said with menace, and the icy glint in his eyes returned. Abe nodded and followed Alex's instruction.

"Open the window, Abe. It's too stuffy in this pit."

Reles walked over to the sash and heaved the pane of glass up. The drapes fluttered in the breeze and both men took a moment to enjoy the fresh air against their faces. In that instant, Abe bolted for the exit but Alex was too quick. Three paces and he reached Reles' hand on the handle and grabbed the guy's wrist, yanking it away from its grip.

Maintaining his hold on Reles, Alex punched the man in the jaw with his fist, which stopped Abe from struggling. Alex dragged him over to the sash and stuffed the gun into his pants pocket. With both hands free, he took Reles by the scruff of the neck.

"Perch on the windowsill, Abe."

A clear instruction issued with no hint of emotion, which Reles followed without hesitation, his legs dangling outside.

"Does it have to be like this, Alex? We both hate Buchalter and Anastasia."

Alex took half a pace back before pushing Reles with all his might, and the guy launched out into the blackness and landed with a crack on the flat roof of the lower building, some fifteen feet away from the side.

"Abe, when you sing like a canary, you must learn to fly like a bird."

6

AS ALEX STOOD in front of the information display at Penn, he was reminded of Meyer's parting words to him. While a plane ride to Cuba sounded exotic, Alex did not like the thought of flying, but a train journey to Vegas and the chance to catch up with an old friend would be a most welcome diversion before he returned to his hovel in LA.

"Meyer, it's me."

"Hello."

"That job has been taken care of."

"Good, and thank you. I will show my appreciation before the end of the day."

"Always glad to help… Before you hang up, could you put me in touch with Benny? I think I might pay him a visit on the way home."

"Sure thing. I'll place a call now and get him to pick you up when you arrive in town."

"You're a mensch."

"So they say."

WHEN ALEX STEPPED off the train in Vegas, there was no one on the platform. Maybe Meyer hadn't kept his word, or perhaps Benny wasn't as pleased to be associated with him as Meyer had implied.

He sighed and wandered toward the exit and out into the arrivals area. The hustle and bustle of the transportation hub overwhelmed him as men and women jostled against him. It was worse than being at Penn.

He made his way to the grand entranceway enjoying the breeze on his face. Then out of the corner of his eye was a guy in a charcoal suit and black hat who was edging toward the door at about the same rate as him. Nothing unusual about that—apart from the fact that the fella had been waiting by the platform exit when he stepped off the train. His back stiffened as he poised himself, ready for action.

A fresh burst of travelers milled through the entranceway and he slipped inside the throng and doubled-back on himself, head down, trying to lower his height and become invisible. He had no idea who the guy was, but he wasn't the welcoming party Alex was expecting. Perhaps Meyer had dropped a dime on him and the syndicate was mopping up old vendettas.

Whatever the reason, Alex found a different way out of the joint. A quick look over his shoulder and the black hat wasn't around. The only trouble was that he was back in the ticketing area, about as close to the center of the building as possible. He ducked into the washrooms, walked into a stall, and shut the door to give himself time to think.

He lit a cigarette and inhaled to clear his mind and consider his options. The washroom entrance opened and closed—there had been two guys at the sinks, and at least one cubicle was locked, with a man standing at the urinal. Then a faucet was turned on and water gurgled. Nothing to worry about on that account.

Alex figured he should remain fifteen minutes and then head straight out. Black hat would have assumed he had lost him leaving the station and, in that case, there would be no point staying here to wait for a fella who had already departed.

A second cigarette consumed, he opened the cubicle to see a different mix of men by the sinks, so he headed out of the room to make a bid for freedom.

◆ ◆ ◆

ALEX STEPPED INTO the main atrium and took two paces forward before a voice he recognized punctured the air.

"Got a smoke, Mac?"

He froze, and as he turned around, he placed his hand in his pants pocket to hold his pistol. By the time he faced back to the washroom, he saw the guy with the black hat and charcoal gray suit, head down, wearing a fedora. The only visible part of his face was the tip of his nose, and that gave Alex no clue who it was—but the voice.

He walked straight up to the fella and pulled out a packet of cigarettes from his jacket. Then he tapped the end of the pack to encourage a single smoke to rise out of the packet and offered it to the guy.

"Thanks, Alex. I don't suppose you've got a light as well?"

Alex smiled at his former lieutenant, Ezra Kohut, and fished out a book of matches with a picture of a half-moon on the front from another pocket.

"Keep 'em."

They shook hands and as they did, Alex placed a palm on Ezra's elbow to show the warmth of his feelings—he hadn't seen this fella since the judge pronounced his sentence.

"If you're here to whack me, better make it quick because I am damn hungry, Ezra."

"What're you talking about? Benny sent me to pick you up, but you've been running around the station ever since you got off the train. When you U-turned into the john I reckoned either you had an upset stomach or you thought you were being followed. So I waited —you had to leave the head at some point."

"Where are you taking me?"

"Benny's in a joint called the El Rancho."

"What kind of place is that?"

"You'll see, Alex. My car's parked outside."

ALEX HAD SEEN nothing like El Rancho before. His life on the east and west coasts—and occasional trips to Chicago and Detroit— meant the Tex-Mex experience had passed him by. The hotel oozed southern state charm, if you liked that kind of thing and cosmopolitan Alex was not such a person.

Ezra saw his expression as they drove into the parking lot and laughed. "This ain't no Richardson, that's for sure."

Mention of their old speakeasy sent an image flashing through Alex's head as he recalled his first date with his mistress, Ida, and the magic of that evening. Then a shudder down his spine as the memory of her limbs flailing as he suffocated her all those years later.

"Times change. People change."

As they approached the entrance on foot, the doorman nodded at Ezra and took him to one side for a quiet word before they reached the lobby. His former lieutenant must have some juice here.

Through the reception area, which could be mistaken for a cantina, crammed as it was with tables for the patrons and enough adobe pots to grow a cactus for every day of the year. Through a restaurant and out onto a patio laden with more adobe-based items and two grins at a table overlooking the pool.

"Good to see you, Alex."

"Likewise, Benny."

"Do you remember Massimo?"

"How will I ever forget my best Italian lieutenant from our New York escapades?"

Handshakes and hugs all round. Then they sat down and Benny Siegel ordered drinks as they jawed about East Coast times and the syndicate. Ezra and Massimo remained quiet during this because they were in the presence of two fellas who were or had been members of the nationwide board which ruled all major organized gangs in the country.

The glasses emptied and were filled again by the attentive waiters while the conversation turned toward the present day.

"How long have you been here, Benny?"

"I moved to LA two years after you journeyed upstate, but as you know I had visited many times before then. Hooked up with Jack Dragna and we did some work together. Last year I heard about what Vegas has to offer and thought I'd check it out for myself. Three weeks later, I relocated and have been here ever since."

"You're attracted to Tex-Mex fakery?"

"I know, but looks can be deceiving. If you strip away the pathetic attempt to mimic Texan casinos, what you have here is a goldmine waiting to be dug."

"Here we go again."

"Listen to me, Alex. All those years ago, did I not say we needed to find a new territory to plunder? Las Vegas is that place."

"And how far have you got following your dream?"

"I'm doing fine. This joint is just the start. I am learning the ropes and figuring out what'll work here for gambling."

"You told me you only needed a piece of green baize and a pack of cards and you'd set up a casino in a week."

"True, but I want more than a mere gaming house. I've got my eyes on a much bigger prize. Imagine a building where there are card tables, for sure, but also we provide a vast array of other entertainment opportunities—restaurants, bars, stage shows, and a room to lay your head so you can stay in the place for days at a time."

Alex recalled his own vision for his speakeasies when he combined drinking, whoring, and a cabaret show. He and Benny weren't far apart if he was honest with himself.

"I've been to Texas and seen how successful the ranch casinos have been and I want to do something similar here—but I realize I can do it better by making my venue more cosmopolitan. We both know that no New Yorker would come to a place that looks as though William Boyd is just around the corner."

"Do you own the El Rancho then?"

"No, not yet. Since coming here, I've spent my time taking control of some hotel services, like prostitution, skimming, and union extortion. Work was going so well that Meyer suggested Ezra and Massimo joined me, and as you were otherwise engaged, I invited them to stay in Vegas."

"Has he been looking after you?"

"Yes, Alex."

"A joke, Massimo. I'd expect no less of Benny, but I am glad matters have worked out for you guys—I never prepared you for my departure."

"Don't worry about it, Alex. Once you went upstate, Ezra and I carried on looking after our ventures under Meyer's watchful eye and protection."

Another round of drinks appeared on the table and Benny proposed a toast. "We live together, we love together…"

"…and we die alone," came the chorus from the others.

"Do you fancy joining the party, Alex? A man of your caliber will make his mark real easily, and there is a tremendous amount we can do in this town. There is no syndicate here—no other gangs jostling for territory. It's like the Bowery all over again. Work with me, Alex."

He weighed up his options in the time it took him to inhale.

"Come back after Hanukkah and we'll make big money together."

January 1942

7

BENNY HELPED ALEX find a place to stay after he arrived in Las Vegas with two suitcases and a pocket full of hope for the future. He had spent his time in LA treading water—not drowning, but not getting anywhere either. He considered that he had survived and that summed up his life from the moment he stepped on the bus that took him to Rikers back in '36.

Living in the City of Angels had been a monotonous experience. His apartment had been somewhere to sleep and eat. Without his ties to New York and the powerful friends he had counted on all his adult life, Alex felt adrift, and to make matters worse, the fire in his belly that drove him to succeed appeared to have been extinguished.

Meeting Benny and some of the old gang showed Alex the world continued to turn and that there was an opportunity out there for the taking. There were no sidewalks paved with gold on offer, but there never were. The only way to succeed is to seize the moment with both hands and not let go until you have squeezed the life out of it, just as he had done to his mistress. May Ida rest in peace.

The place Benny found for him was a block away from the corner of Las Vegas Boulevard and Sahara Avenue, the location of the El Rancho. Alex's third-floor apartment came with two bedrooms and a view of the desert—almost every joint in the city had a sandy vista because the town comprised only two streets and a handful of stores, along with a sprawled out residential area. And the funny thing was that Alex could walk to work because he was stationed at the El Rancho with an official job title of services manager, a phrase so meaningless not even Benny could remember why he chose it.

"You'll get a name badge and a regular paycheck, but you will earn through me too."

"Just make sure you provide me with enough documentation for my income statement to the IRS."

"And you used to accuse me of making jokes."

"Benny, I am dead serious. Every year since I left the joint, I have filed my taxes. There is no way they will drag me back to jail."

"Sure, Alex, but remember that if we are only half as successful as I predict, you will make much more than any hotel worker could generate."

"I'll figure something out when the time comes."

"You do that, Alex. Meantime, pop over to El Rancho's restaurant tomorrow afternoon. A friend of mine is coming into town I want you to meet."

"ALEX, THIS IS Mickey. You share two things so I know you'll get along. First, there's your name—you are both Cohens."

"And second, Benny?"

"You were both boxers. What are the odds, right?"

Alex shook hands with the stocky balding man a handful of years his junior and the three men sat down. He had a firm grip and a keen eye, but his abdomen had gone to seed since his glory days in the ring a decade before.

When Benny first headed west, he had worked alongside Dragna, eventually usurping his top-dog position. Then Benny brought in Mickey over Dragna's head, who remained unforgiving of the whole escapade–one reason Mickey was so eager to come to Vegas.

Alex didn't care about what had happened on the west coast—he knew Benny well enough from days gone by to understand how the fella operated. He blew hot and cold in the same breath. One minute the world was a joke, the next he'd hold a gun to a guy's head and shoot his brains clean out.

"The first thing we need to do is get this joint here sorted out. The name on the deed may not be mine, but I want to ensure that I dip my beak in every available trough."

"Benny, what do you want us to do?"

"Alex, you and Mickey should start with the hotel workers. Most of them are unionized—I do not judge—but we need to control this Hotel and Restaurant Employees Union. Nothing we do in El Rancho will succeed without the staff."

THE TWO MEN used the rest of the afternoon to sip coffees, get to know each other better, and form a plan of attack.

"I heard you worked with Capone back in the day."

"Yes, Alex. I spent a while in Chicago with Alfonse during the early years of Prohibition. Good guy. I got a lot of time for him and his brother."

"I never met a sibling."

"Mattie's a decent fella too. Quieter than Alfonse, but bright as a button."

"That makes both of them then. You heard anything about how Alfonse is doing?"

"Didn't you know? They put him into Alcatraz and then three years ago they paroled him. Word on the street is that he's a gibbering idiot—potatoes for brains. I met a guy who'd spoken to a fella who said Alfonse was retired in Florida waiting to die."

"He took a beating in Alcatraz?"

"Apparently not. Some medical condition or he just turned plain stupid. A couple of the old-timers think it's only an act to keep him out of jail, but I know for a fact that he went into hospital in Baltimore so I'm not so sure about that."

Alex mulled over what Mickey had said. If he ever got a chance, he'd head down to Florida and try to visit the guy. They weren't the closest of friends but jail, hospital, and a slow death weren't how Alfonse should meet his end. The man deserved a hail of bullets or a sudden heart attack on top of his wife or mistress. Not to lose his mind and fade into obscurity under the Miami-Dade sun.

◆ ◆ ◆

ALEX, MICKEY, EZRA, and Massimo got to work the next day when they tracked down the local convener folding sheets in the laundry room. Hughie Mathews had constructed a fine pile of white cotton blankets before the four men surrounded him. He jumped as he looked up–their footsteps had been hidden under the clatter of the nearby machinery.

"Are you Hughie?"

The guy eyed Alex, unsure whether this was a shakedown, but certain he didn't recognize two of the group.

"Yes. Forgive me, I know Mr. Kohut and Mr. Sciarra, but we have not been introduced."

"I am Mr. Cohen, but call me Alex."

"And I am Mr. Cohen, which is why you should call me Mickey."

Mathews smiled at the lightness of touch and then his face soured as he reminded himself that Ezra and Massimo were in the group. Everybody knew they were with Benny Siegel, and that man was a gangster.

"How can I help you? I doubt if you've gained an interest in the cleaning services offered at the hotel."

"Hughie, you are right. We don't give a damn about the sheets, but we care about your members. When you get a chance, would you be so kind as to join us for a refreshment on the veranda?"

"Will there be liquor to drink?"

"If you want."

"Then I'll see you in an hour when I have my break."

"You can take it now if you'd prefer."

"Is that on the up and up, Mr. Kohut?"

"Sure, bud. Call me Ezra."

◆ ◆ ◆

"THIS IS THE situation as I understand it, Hughie."

Alex had ordered everyone a beer, which Mathews consumed with relish. This was a working stiff who grabbed any opportunity that came his way.

"The El Rancho does its best to look after its staff, but it doesn't offer top-dollar wages and it could do better with sick pay. No disrespect to Ezra and Massimo who have been helping Mr. Siegel in the place for a while now, as I understand it."

"You new to town?"

"Came out this month and Mickey arrived yesterday, before you ask."

"Must be something big happening if such important men as you are crawling out of the woodwork."

Alex glanced at Mickey, who returned the gesture with a slight curling of his mouth. Mathews might be a small-time union sap, but he wasn't as stupid as he first appeared.

"We think the union can do better for itself and we would like to help. Would you be willing to accept two new members?"

"Always happy for people to pay their dues."

"We would expect to receive complimentary membership."

Mathews almost spat out a mouthful of beer.

"Now I think I've heard everything."

"Hear me out, Hughie. By having Mickey and me as representatives, you are very unlikely to find you have any problems with the hotel administration. In fact, I will provide my personal guarantee that is the case."

"We might only have been open for less than a year, but we have had no trouble yet with the management, so your offer doesn't mean very much."

"Hughie, my friend. You are looking at the past while Mickey and I are staring at the future coming down the tracks. James Cashman and Thomas Hull are fine men as management goes, but as time passes, you will find they'll need to cut corners to maximize their profit. And we all know that the first people to get it in the neck are the employees, right?"

"I guess… but why would Ezra and Massimo want to side with us workers when they've stood by Cashman and Hull since the place opened?"

"We represent outside interests, Hughie."

Ezra spoke softly, slowly, and his eyes were stone cold boring into Mathews' soul.

"I'm still not sure. You're selling tonic water to a healthy man."

"Hughie, let me make it easier for you. If you don't accept our invitation to help, then be certain of one thing: you will not be able to protect your members from the risks that prowl in every corner of a hotel. Who knows what accidents may befall an individual as they walk past this pool on the slippery surface of this patio…"

"Or what dangers lurk in the laundry machinery. Whoops, how did Hughie's hand get caught in the vicelike grip of that press?" Mickey offered this prediction while cracking his knuckles and that made Mathews swallow hard.

"Welcome to the union, gentlemen."

"Thank you. And one other thing—each Friday you will provide us with a small payment, let's say fifty dollars initially."

"What the hell for?"

"To protect you and your members from all these unforeseen circumstances we just mentioned."

"How am I going to afford that?"

"We are not asking you to put your hand into your pocket. That would be unjust. Raise your membership fees—that's what I would do if I were you."

8

ON FRIDAY, ALEX found Hughie in the laundry room, emptying large baskets of dirty clothing for sorting. Mathews caught sight of him early on this time, and Alex swore the man sighed from two hundred feet—shoulders raised and then slumped downward. He pretended not to notice Alex's impending arrival, but as soon as they were within shouting distance, Hughie nodded and stopped what he was doing.

"How's your week been?"

"Quiet, thanks, Alex."

"Just shows you what happens when Mickey and I get involved in the union."

"Yeah, right."

"Do you have the appreciation we asked for?"

Hughie nodded again and put his hand in a pocket to retrieve a bundle of notes. Alex counted the green and handed back a dollar.

"We are not thieves. I'm not going to stiff you, even over a single greenback."

"Mighty upright of you."

"Hughie, we are starting a long-term relationship and this journey best begins with each of us trusting the other. If we don't have that then we've got nothing."

"And I want you to understand that cash came from my pocket—I cannot ask my men to fund your theft."

"Harsh words, Hughie. Before you go slinging mud around, you better make sure you are on safe ground, my friend."

"Extracting money with menaces—that's extortion."

"I have not threatened you, Hughie, and I will not take kindly to anyone who spreads those kinds of rumors about me. Do you understand?"

Alex stepped one pace forward so that their noses were only inches apart–the fear in Mathews' eyes and the beads of sweat coagulating across his forehead.

"I told you before, if you prefer to have an easy time, raise membership fees. With the number of workers in this joint, adding a quarter on the current levy will get you my money and keep everyone nice and safe. There is no need for you to end up on poverty row for the sake of the staff here. You won't want it, the members wouldn't want that, and I have no use for you if you are destitute."

Alex leaned back to give Hughie some thinking space because the aim was to get the guy onside, not to intimidate him into making foolish decisions.

"I'm not sure they could all afford that."

"Then consider going on strike and demand more pay—nickel an hour would more than cover the extra and everyone would be happy —apart from Cashman and Hull. If they can manage to spend half a million to build this joint then the company should pay everybody a nickel more, right?"

"But nobody wants to lose a day's wage striking."

"It won't go that far. Remember, Mickey and I are on your side. A bit of chest-puffing negotiation and they will cave. You have my word on that."

Hughie smiled for the first time since he'd received a free beer. "Looks like we might get along just swell."

"For sure… and another thing before I forget, in the next week or two you'll have some more complimentary members. I'm increasing the number of working women in the resort and the union must get behind them from day one."

✦ ◆ ✦

WHEN THE GIRLS arrived, Mathews needed no introductions–he spotted the nafkas a mile away.

"Hughie, if you want this hotel to thrive, we need to occupy our guests all the time. So we'll send families on a horse ride in the day and offer the men experiences of the flesh without their wives and kids."

"Alex, sometimes two blackjack tables, a roulette wheel, one craps table, and three rows of slot machines aren't enough."

"Playing cards is more fun when there's a woman on your arm and the promise of happiness at the end of your weary day."

Mickey understood that men liked to gamble and would do so on the spin of a coin. The local families who owned most of the real estate in the city took a piece of the action from each of the guys who ran a book in their bars and Mickey wanted to dip his beak in the same trough. So he went around the joints nearest to El Rancho to convince them to bend to his will.

The former boxer used a variety of means of persuasion, but by the time Alex's first call girls arrived in town, Mickey was getting ten percent from each venue. Then he turned his attention to El Rancho itself.

"You reckon the casino is as successful as it could be, Alex?"

"There's always room for improvement, but I think we need to watch the croupiers before we worry about anything else."

"Damn straight. I observed them all last night. Every single one is skimming from the take, and each croupier is palming cards and fixing winners."

"Let's both go tonight and find out if we can make everybody see reason."

ALEX AND MICKEY met up at ten to give the room a chance to get swinging. Massimo and Ezra were also there, but Alex had instructed them to keep their distance otherwise they'd be too easily spotted.

The advantage the two Cohens had was that they were both new in the hotel and not everyone had seen who they were. Alex's old lieutenants were all too well known. One Scotch later and Mickey nudged Alex and eyed a guy on a blackjack table. Alex nodded and they sauntered over to watch the game unfold.

Three men sat in front of the dealer, and to the casual observer, everything looked peachy. Nobody appeared to be winning more than the others, and the cards seemed to ebb and flow as a game of chance should.

To a more trained eye, each round involved at least one card being dealt from the bottom of the deck. Alex leaned in to speak into Mickey's ear in a hushed tone, "Middle player. Every time he exchanges money for chips, he gets more than he has paid for. They're working together."

"Yeah and he's winning way more hands than the other two. I'm surprised the other players haven't noticed."

"They're good. The dealer makes sure his accomplice loses enough small hands that it feels fair."

They stepped back and watched some more. Alex was impressed with Averill Cartwright's technique as he carried on dealing. A single finger raised in the air got Ezra to scoot around the edge of the room and pass by.

"When the middle client leaves, follow him out and don't let him leave the hotel. We need a conversation—bring your knuckleduster."

Ezra returned to his station near Massimo and shared the instruction before they split up to cover both exits—one to the lobby and the other to the guest rooms. There was nothing to do but watch and wait. An hour later and the other two card sharps gave up on the night and headed out. Within thirty seconds, the middle player cashed out and walked away without leaving a tip. Most unusual. Alex joined the guy and Mickey approached Averill.

The card sharp went up to the reception desk and asked for his key.

"There you go, Mr. Eady. Have a good night."

The beaming grin of the receptionist was met with a half-smile by Hollis Eady, who turned around to head to the stairs but faced Alex instead.

"I wonder if you'd mind spending two minutes helping us find out what our customers think of the hotel?"

"Not right now, Mac. I'm heading up to bed—it's been a long day."

"I understand, but I must insist you help El Rancho improve its customer experience."

Alex seized Eady's elbow with a vicelike grip and dragged the man across the lobby and through a side door then down the corridor of this staff-only area and into a room with a table and a few chairs and not much else—apart from Averill already sitting down along with Mickey, Ezra, and Massimo. Alex threw Hollis into a seat next to Averill, ensuring the force of the movement was too great, so he nearly toppled over as soon as he landed on the chair.

"You need to listen and you must listen good, the pair of you."

Alex pointed at both men while Ezra took out his knuckleduster and wrapped it around his fist. Hollis' and Averill's eyes followed Ezra's actions, but the way their eyeballs flitted toward him told Alex they were listening too.

"We will not tolerate people stealing from us at El Rancho—whether that is the staff or a patron."

"We done nothing…"

Averill didn't have time to finish his sentence because Ezra punched him in the jaw. Hollis' mouth gaped open and his breathing went into overdrive. A tooth landed on the table and splatters of Averill's blood reached Hollis' sleeve.

"This is not a discussion. This is a situation where you need to listen. Understand?"

Both men nodded and Alex continued.

"How much money you make tonight, Mr. Eady?"

"Dunno, mister. A couple of hundred."

"Empty your pockets and give me two C-notes."

Eady shoved his hands in his pants and jacket until he remembered where he kept his roll, and then he counted out the required amount. Mickey saw how much the guy had remaining in his hand and snatched the rest of Eady's bundle.

"And this is the money you owe me, you *gonif*."

"I've got nothing left."

Alex laughed and Mickey chuckled in reaction.

"We are leaving you with your life, little man… Massimo, please show this gentleman the way out. He's departing the hotel immediately so take him up to his room and help him pack. He needs to be gone in less than five minutes."

"Where will I go at this time of night?"

"Not my problem."

Massimo hustled Hollis out of the door as Averill sweated buckets.

"We watched you steal from us throughout the evening, Cartwright."

"It was Hollis' idea—I just needed the money. He told me that if we played fast and loose, then we could both make a little extra on the side."

"How many days you been playing this game?"

"It's the third night—and it was to be the last anyway, honest. You gotta believe me."

Mickey slugged him in the face and blood gushed out of his nose. Just before he delivered another punch to the dealer, Alex put a hand on his arm.

"Your punishment is that you will lose your job and I never want to see you again. Not in the hotel. If you notice me walking down Fremont then you turn and go the other way. Do you understand?"

"Yessir."

"Good. Ezra, please escort this thief from the premises and give him his severance pay."

His lieutenant looked confused for a minute until Alex explained. "Give him what we owe him." A raise of an eyebrow and Ezra got the picture—he buried Cartwright's body a mile out in the desert an hour after Averill's departure from the hotel.

Within a day, word had leaked out about the dealer's disappearance and the sudden exit of Hollis Eady from El Rancho. Mickey had no problems with skimming in the casino from that moment on.

FEBRUARY 1942

9

ONE INNOVATION EL Rancho brought to Las Vegas was what it called its Opera House. While Caruso had been dead twenty years, the venue was not aimed at his kind of performance. Instead, it offered a run-of-the-mill stage show, featuring a mix of singing, dancing, and joke telling—vaudeville in all but name.

The setup reminded Alex of what he had done at the Richardson blind pig when he needed to find a way of increasing early evening takings—during the time slot between the afternoon gamblers and nighttime whoremongers. A headline act would appear for a week and then drift away to an off-Broadway run in New York or back to Los Angeles and its theater district. In between was the Opera House and its audience of men seeking some respite from their losses at the casino.

Alex was no expert in the performing arts, but he knew what he liked, and time in the Opera House after work diverted his attention from his loneliness when he returned to his apartment to sleep. While the comedians' jokes didn't always hit their mark, they were more funny than not. The singers were passable and the hoofers moved well enough around the stage.

Thoughts of the performances in the Richardson took Alex's mind to Ida, his mistress, and then to her sorry demise. She had been the toast of Yiddish theater in her day, but that day was a long time ago in a city far away.

He liked to sit near the back of the auditorium so he could slink off whenever he wanted without getting in the way of any of the customers. He also believed it gave him the best view of the sweep of the stage on the rare occasion when the director did more than get the actors to stand in the center and bellow out their lines.

A comedian left—none too soon in Alex's opinion—and a lone woman skipped to the center and sang. The band joined in after the first phrase and then the Opera House filled up with a variety of dancers, all jiggling about in unison. Toes were tapping in the audience and Alex made a mental note they should hang onto the singer because the crowd liked her.

As the song drew to a climax, the chorus fluttered in front of the lead and returned to the wings to let the star shine in all her glory. That was the moment he almost dropped his Scotch. The fourth girl in the line looked familiar—her face, at any rate. He racked his brains to place where he had seen her before.

Perhaps he'd noticed her out of the corner of his eye, walking around the hotel or on the sidewalk—that was the most obvious answer. Maybe she'd been in Los Angeles and they'd bumped into each other there. While that was possible, it didn't chime with Alex. Then the answer slapped him in the kisser.

The last time he had seen the woman was in New York about twenty years ago when he was recuperating from the war and he and Sarah had gone out to a show. He'd seen her then for less than a second, but his heart had all but exploded out of his chest. And Alex was feeling the same response now. Singing and dancing at the back of the stage was his childhood sweetheart, Rebecca. He beckoned a waitress over.

"How long before the show's finished?"

"It's not that bad, is it?"

"No, I'd like to introduce myself to a member of the cast and don't want to be in the way until the performance has ended."

The waitress gave him a knowing smile and bent down so she could be heard over the music.

"The whole enchilada will be cooked in another ten minutes—fifteen at most. Would you like me to buy some flowers to offer her?"

"That'd be great. Could you?"

"I was joking, Mr. Cohen, but I'll see what I can do."

"Sorry, my mistake. Don't go to any bother on my account."

By the time the audience applauded all the performers as they took their final bows, Alex was standing too and clapping as loud as he was able, causing the occasional head to turn. He didn't care. He collected the bunch of red roses the waitress had acquired for him and headed for the stage door.

ALEX FOUGHT HIS way through all the acts as they tumbled into the narrow corridor which led backstage. First there was a closed door with a silver star on the front, and then there were a series of other changing rooms—some small, others large—and dozens of men and women casting off their costumes and make-up.

He checked out each room until he reached the far end of the corridor and the last door. Girls streamed in and out, which made him guess this was the location of the chorus line. He pushed open the door with his foot to preserve his roses and popped his head inside.

His eyes almost bulged out of his skull—Alex had never seen so much bare female flesh on display at once. And that included his time running Lower East Side prostitution for most of the twenties and half of the thirties.

"Hey, Mac, close your mouth and shut the door. If you want to stay here, we charge for a late show."

"Don't be like that. The john's got a bunch of flowers. He might be about to ask you for a date."

The two women cackled with laughter at Alex's expense, but he ignored them. Instead, he kept searching around the room for Rebecca. Three minutes later, he reckoned he had checked out every face in the place apart from one. It was hidden inside a dress that refused to go on over the owner's head; she had decided not to undo the neck before changing.

Alex stepped forward, at which point the unknown woman spun round with her elbows sticking out hoping a rotating motion would ease the transport of a skull through a hole which was too small. An elbow thumped into Alex, causing him to step to one side and to drop the roses on the ground. In response to bumping into an uncharted and unexpected body, the girl bounced in the opposite direction and landed on the floor, legs in the air with her panties visible to the world.

He bent down and took her by the arm while unzipping her dress by about five inches—more than enough to free her from her torment. "Thanks, Mac," she said without looking at who had given her liberty.

When she glanced at Alex, she stopped herself in her tracks and squinted at him. Then her cheeks went red and she sat up to regain her composure.

"Alex?"

He nodded and put out a hand to help Rebecca to her feet.

"What the fuck are you doing here?"

"I could ask the same of you, Rebecca."

"I work here. And you?"

"Me too. I pulled into town a few weeks ago and thought I'd catch a show before I went home."

"We arrived last night—and ship out tomorrow."

"In that case, let me buy you a drink—unless you have anyone waiting for you in the wings."

"I got nobody, Alex."

AT THEIR POOLSIDE table, he ordered another Scotch and Rebecca chose a Southside—gin and mint on the rocks in a tumbler. They chinked glasses and settled in for their conversation.

"You always yearned to become a dancer—all those hours practicing in your parents' apartment have come good."

"You're kind, Alex. Ever since I was a little girl, I wanted to dance and that's what I've been doing for the last twenty years—been stuck in the chorus line of second-rate shows across the country."

"I might not be an expert, but I recall you had genuine talent."

"In this business, it's not how well you can dance but who you'll sleep with that counts the most. And I won't put it about for just anyone."

Rebecca stared straight into Alex's eyes as she mouthed the last phrase. Was she implying that she maintained her high morals from their teenage years or was giving him a massive come-on? He only knew he had spent his life not understanding women at all well.

"You're doing something you enjoy, which is more than most of the saps round here can say. I mean, the customers here spend their lives earning money to gamble it away in a matter of hours and then return to their miserable jobs to repeat the process until the next year."

"That's entertainment."

She giggled at her own joke and looked round to find a waiter to refill her glass. Nobody appeared until Alex raised an eye and then a fresh Southside materialized pronto.

"Here's to you, Alex Cohen. I saw your name in the papers a while back and drank a beer to your memory. Since then, zip."

Alex swirled his drink in its glass, letting the ice whoosh round the sides, before answering.

"I've had my difficulties—like my trial five years ago. Uncle Sam wasn't happy about the amount of tax I'd paid."

"They threw you in jail, right?"

"Yeah, but that's behind me and I'm making a living in Vegas, working with some people I knew back in New York."

"I always told you I didn't want to mix with criminal types."

"You used to taunt me about my business." Rebecca laughed.

"Yes. Your cheeks turned a funny shade of crimson when I shamed you about your gangster friends. I couldn't help myself."

"I was on top of the world, Rebecca, before my trial."

"And here you are in Vegas, watching second-rate shows with third-rate actresses."

"Don't say that about yourself. Even if you haven't, I always believed in you."

"Always? During the two decades since we saw each other and I told you I wanted nothing to do with you while you were…"

"…sleeping with Sarah, who later became my wife."

"Wow. Forgive me—I never treated you fairly. I was too young to know what *momzers* were out there, to appreciate what I almost had."

"It is easy to be wise in hindsight."

"You have any children?"

"Five boys."

"Still married?"

"No, I divorced her before I went inside. She's in Hoboken along with the kids. They haven't flown far from the nest."

"Look, Alex, it's getting late and I've an early train to catch…"

"You don't have to explain. It was great talking to you, if only for a few minutes."

"You interrupted me. I was going to say that I have to run tomorrow and would like to invite you back to my place but I'm sharing a room with three other girls and that is not the after drinks party I had in mind. You got somewhere we could go?"

"My apartment's a five-minute walk away."

"Then what are we still doing here? We have a lot more… talking to do before the night is through."

"I know this is early in the conversation, but I'll put it out there. I have some juice with the management and can get you a full-time, hundred-dollar-a-week contract at the drop of a hat. Front of house, not in the chorus."

"First, let's go to your bed before we make any long-term plans."

"You've changed, Rebecca."

"Like you can't imagine."

She patted him on the arm and they strolled through the lobby and out onto the sidewalk.

MAY 1942

10

"I HAVE MY eye on a piece of land, Mickey."

"Alex, is that why we are standing in the parking lot of the 91 Club, in the middle of nowhere, a mile south of El Rancho?"

"Pretty much. There's talk that some Texan movie theater owner wants to build a casino here, and I want some of that action."

"What's stopping you?"

"A fella you might know from LA who's holding out on a price—Guy McAfee."

Mickey raised a smile and nodded.

"Guy and I go back a ways. He was captain of the vice squad and left town to run this joint when a new mayor arrived in the city. This looks a classic McAfee dive—unpleasant to the eye but serves a mean drink. Shall we find out?"

"I'm not in the mood for a beer, Mickey. There are a few matters I need to sort out, but if I can get things arranged right, would you like to share the investment with me?"

"Why not do this alone?"

"Because it pays to have friends and besides, you and I have worked well together this past year and I prefer to spread success. I wouldn't want you to think I tried to prevent you from making a pile of dough. Resentment does unpleasant things to a man's mind."

"Thank you, Alex. I appreciate your concern and generosity. Right now, I am cash poor and so I can't take up your offer. Unlike some, I didn't make millions out of Prohibition."

"Any fool can generate a million—keeping it is the hard part. Between my ex-wife and Sing Sing, you'd be surprised how little I have left."

"Especially as your new skirt has been hanging around for quite a while now. I doubt if her apartment was cheap."

"I've looked after Rebecca and don't you worry how much rent I pay each month."

ALEX'S PROBLEM WAS simple: like almost every business deal in Vegas, there was always a local family that had an interest and who needed to be accommodated before any handshake could occur. In the case of the real estate surrounding the 91 Club, there was the slight matter of the planning office. The leader of the committee, Jackson Garnett was also the brother of the county sheriff, Woodie— the soil was outside the city line so Benny had no influence over those local yokels.

For any transfer of ownership to run smoothly, Alex needed to grease the wheels of bureaucracy and he was happy to do that. If he was prepared to bribe Tammany Hall officials, sending a wad of notes to a pinhead in Nevada would not be a moral issue for him.

Yet this was Alex's problem. Jackson was a weak individual who'd spent his entire adult life refusing to think for himself. In any other managerial job, this would be a major hindrance, but the land office operated in a different way. Jackson did nothing without the approval of his older brother, and Woodie did nothing without a good reason.

"THANKS FOR SEEING me, Sheriff Garnett."

"Always pleased to meet concerned citizens, Mr. *Cohen*."

Had Garnett emphasized his name to remember it or because he wanted to stress the Jewishness of the word? Alex let it go for now and focused on the purpose of his visit to the policeman's office.

"I am hoping you can help me with a situation that has arisen."

"We like to serve the community, Mr. Cohen."

"Call me Alex. There's a tract of land I'm interested in purchasing, but I am concerned that the sale won't get through the onerous vetting process from the county office."

"Well, I don't see how I can help you with that, Alex. I'm here to uphold the law, not stamp pieces of paper."

He chuckled because he knew why Alex was here and what he wanted. For reasons best known to himself, he was making things difficult for this man stood in front of him, while he slouched in his chair with his feet resting on the desk.

"As you know how the wheels turn so well around these parts, I thought you would help me secure safe passage for my endeavor."

"They might let your kind buy land in Vegas, boy, but your sort are not welcome in my county."

Alex inhaled to stop himself from taking immediate action, tipped his hat, and left the police station.

MICKEY JOINED ALEX that night and sat in his automobile until Jackson locked up and plodded to his vehicle. With Alex behind the wheel, they tailed Garnett's car until it stopped in the parking lot of the 91 Club. The fat dude disgorged himself and propped up the bar for a beer or two.

"What do you want to do, Alex?"

"We wait. There's no conversation we can have with him in front of a bar full of witnesses. I am hoping to convince him to help us without grandstanding before a bunch of drunks."

Almost an hour after Mickey asked his question, Jackson staggered out of the bar and into his car. Then he lurched out of the lot and back onto the highway. Alex followed at a safe distance for two miles south of Vegas when the cop left the road and parked in front of the Nevada Ring motel and entered a room, which opened just as he arrived at the door.

"Our sheriff was expected."

"Could you tell if it was a woman, Mickey?"

"Not for certain, but do you think Garnett is meeting a man in the middle of the night at this rundown shack?"

"I was thinking it might be a poker game. Nothing more sordid than that."

They hopped out and scurried to the motel and followed the frontage over to Jackson's room. Alex bent by the draped window and tried to look through the sliver of a gap. Then he stood up and walked over to Mickey, flattened to the wall next to the jamb.

"He ain't going nowhere for a few minutes at least, Mickey."

They smoked a cigarette and then Alex knocked on the door. A few mumbled words came from inside, but nobody welcomed them in. Mickey shrugged and kicked the door in with one well-aimed heel to the lock.

The sheriff and a woman were naked on top of the bed and from what Alex saw, satisfaction had yet to be achieved for either party.

"What the...?"

"Sheriff Garnett, so good to see you again. And you must be Mrs. Garnett, I presume?"

The woman struggled to grab a corner of the blanket to hide her embarrassment, but the lump of a cop was more concerned with protecting his own dignity. She looked at Jackson and then switched her attention back to Alex.

"I'm not..."

"Of course you're not married to this, darling." Alex pointed a casual finger at Garnett. "Why would he waste his money on such a crummy motel if you were? I'd advise you to throw your clothes on and get the hell out of here. Pretend this never happened."

Mickey helped by chucking her undies at her while she was still in bed and within a minute Garnett's companion had left the building as the sheriff tried to find his shorts.

"Stay on the mattress, Mr. Garnett. We wouldn't want you to get lost in this sumptuous paradise you built for your queen."

"No need to be all sarcastic, Cohen."

"I told you to call me Alex and I would prefer it if you do. Understand?"

A nod of acquiescence.

"If you recall, earlier today we were discussing a trifling matter of some real estate and I asked for your help and you refused."

"It wasn't like that, Alex."

Mickey slapped the cop on the back. "Don't talk unless you're ordered to, boy."

"You told me you had no influence over your brother and that you didn't want Jews anywhere near your beloved county. Well, now you got two of them in the same room. Does that bother you, sheriff?"

Mickey slapped him on the back again. "Answer the question, boy."

"No, not at all. I was just horsing around with you before. I am sure we can come to an arrangement over that land matter."

Alex faced Mickey and laughed. "Now the *goy* wants to negotiate."

Meanwhile, Jackson tried to slither off the bed and put his shorts on. With one foot inside, Alex turned back to him and pulled out his revolver, aiming it at Garnett's head.

"Stop what you're doing, mister. I did not give you permission to do jack squat."

Mickey lunged over and punched him in the jaw, causing the overweight cop to topple over, with his feet caught up in his underwear. Alex took two paces forward, round the corner of the bed, and placed a hand on Mickey's forearm as he readied to land another punch.

"My friend here wishes you harm but I only seek resolution. Before he gets his way, put on your shorts because the sight of you on the floor with your balls in the air is not something I wish to experience for a second longer than I have to."

Alex waited for Garnett to right himself and sit back on the bed, doing his best to maintain what little dignity remained.

"Does your wife know?"

"About Phyllis? No. I mean, she might suspect something…"

"Let me give you a word of advice, Garnett. She knows. Mine did when I played around and yours will too. The way you walk back into the house after you've visited Phyllis in this motel or the smell of her perfume on your collar. She'll know for sure."

Mickey grinned as Jackson's cheeks reddened. Alex lit a cigarette and threw the match on the floor.

"You must convince your brother to let the sale of the 91 Club land go through without a hitch. If there are any problems or difficulties— if the paperwork gets lost or a signature is missing—then I shall find you and Mickey'll continue what he started tonight."

"And I will only stop when you are dead, you *fercockte dreck*."

"You understand?"

"Yes, Alex."

"Now put your pants on and slink back to your wife. Buy her some flowers and do something nice for her. You don't deserve her, so show some gratitude once in a while."

"Yessir."

Alex and Mickey waited for Jackson to leave the motel and drive off before they left the room.

"Would you have killed him or were you just doing a scare act on him, Mickey?"

"He'd have been dead unless you wanted to save him. I didn't care. Either way, the brother would have seen the deeds through safely."

"Now all I got to do is convince the guys who actually want to buy the land that they need me as an investor and get Guy McAfee to decide he wants to sell."

"I can't help you with the buyers, but tell McAfee that Benny and I say hello. He'll do whatever you ask at that point."

"You got history, huh?"

"Guy ran gambling in LA for Benny, and I was the bagman. We have a shared past."

RICHARD E GRIFFITH was a smart businessman who recognized the opportunity in footfall that Vegas represented. He had selected a location outside the city line but on the way in from Los Angeles on Highway 91 before anybody reached El Rancho. The man had hired his architect nephew, Bill Moore, to draw up plans for the thirty-five-acre site. The only sticking point was that McAfee didn't want to sell for reasonable money. Alex paid Griffith a visit to see what could be arranged.

"Thank you for agreeing to receive me, Mr. Griffith. I appreciate that a man in your position has little time and many people seeking to squander it."

"You are very welcome, Alex, but I asked around and understand you have a certain status in the community, shall we say?"

"Very kind. Now that we have massaged each other's egos, may I be presumptuous and get down to business?"

"A man after my own heart. Do proceed."

"Word on the street is that you are seeking to acquire a piece of land south of Vegas and that McAfee is demanding silly money for the privilege of handing over his ramshackle fleapit of a bar."

"This is true. I want to make the purchase and the toad isn't playing ball."

"What if I told you I am able to not only get McAfee to accept a lowball price but I can guarantee that the county will smooth out any issues which may arise as the paperwork makes its way through the bureaucracy—locals prefer locals buying their real estate."

"Alex, that'd be mighty peachy, but I suppose you'll want something in exchange."

"Correct. I will pay for the land out of my own pocket—I don't foresee it costing more than a thousand anyway—and in return, I would like a thirty percent stake in the hotel complex you and your nephew intend to develop."

"That's a high price you want to charge me."

"The resort will cost money to build and you will fund that, so from the get-go, it'll make a loss. I'm asking for just under a third of an enterprise that'll be worth nothing. And I secure the deal in the first place."

"You are a smooth talker, Alex."

He finished his cigarette and allowed Griffith to mull over the proposition.

"Well?"

"I'd be more comfortable with twenty or even a ten percent stake for you. After all, I have to care for my nephew."

"Look after him as much as you want, but that always comes from your end of the deal. It is thirty percent or nothing. Take it or leave it."

"And if I leave it?"

Alex smiled and flicked a piece of fluff off his pants.

"Then you would lose a business partner and gain an enemy. All my partners have made money. You choose which path to follow, but I want to know before I leave this room today. My time is as precious as yours and I do not intend to wait around on your decision."

Griffith took a puff on his cigar, which had been burning steadily throughout their conversation, and balanced it on the rim of his ashtray. Then he spat in his palm and reached out to shake hands. Alex was about to own a chunk of the Last Frontier hotel and casino. Griffith cracked open a bottle of Scotch to celebrate and they shared a drink before Alex bade him good day and hustled over to McAfee to coerce him into selling for a paltry thousand bucks.

11

JAMES RAGEN HAD a singular vision—to provide the country's only racing wire. The Samaritan figured that if he controlled the only source of competition results to bookies from one coast to the other then he would dictate when anybody heard which horse had won and by how many lengths.

Why would this matter? Because there was money to be made from calculating the odds of an event when you already knew the winner. An unscrupulous bookie could alter the odds he was offering in between the race actually finishing and the result being announced in some hick town on the other side of the country.

Ragen invested in the phone cable and trained up staff to learn how to listen to a stream of racing results and updates while simultaneously writing it all down or dictating it for somebody else to scrawl onto paper. In racetracks where he didn't have the authorization, he'd rent a nearby room and station a guy with a pair of binoculars to read the odds off the tote board by the track. So long as Ragen obtained the information he needed, he did not care how he got it.

Benny Siegel understood the importance of the Nationwide News Service wire and wanted a piece of the action. He had run gambling in Los Angeles with Jack Dragna and Mickey, and he wanted to do the same in Vegas.

"Alex, I have a proposition for you."

"If there's money to be made, I'm all ears."

"Have you come across James Ragen in your travels?"

"Not yet, but I have a feeling that I will do soon."

"Funny, Alex. He owns and runs the Nationwide News Service and if we want to run gambling in this city then we must get our hands on the wire."

"Where does this Ragen live?"

"In Los Angeles last I heard."

"So what do we need him for? We have direct or indirect control of the only casinos in town and Mickey is working his way through all the bookies in the bars here too."

"Alex, sometimes you make me laugh. Running the buildings where gaming takes place is good because the house can charge for the privilege of owning a floor, walls, and a ceiling, but the real money is made by those who set the odds."

"The probabilities are all fixed in a casino, though."

"Unless our dealers are palming cards, yes. The chances of a queen of spades appearing in a pack are the same every time some poor sap plays, Alex."

"But with horses it is different."

"Exactly so. It is one reason many people prefer racing. The unknown is never far away."

"Great if you are a john but not if you're running the book."

"The calculation to price the odds so the house is guaranteed to come out in profit no matter who wins—is much easier if you take the risk out of the process. Knowing the winners minutes before the locals find out is the edge a bookie needs."

The jigsaw pieces fell into place in Alex's mind. They get access to the wire and feed their bookies the results so that the odds can be fixed before the races are over.

"Benny, back to the point then. Why do you want to know if I've met Ragen before?"

"Simple. We must convince him to sell his interest in the Nationwide News Service and between us, I reckon we can do it. To show my confidence in you, I'll offer you a fifty-fifty split of whatever stake we gouge out of him."

"You'd better finish your cocktail. We've got a train to Los Angeles to catch. I never thought I'd hear myself say this, but I can't wait until I get back to the City of Angels."

RAGEN'S OFFICE WAS in Burbank—a much more pleasant corner of town than Alex's old haunts, and the two men waited in the guy's anteroom. Benny had had the foresight to book an appointment because he figured a fella like Ragen would not want to be blindsided by two Vegas hoods.

"Very kind of you to see us, Mr. Ragen."

"Benny, no need to be all formal with me just because you've brought along a new friend."

He eyed Alex for an instant and ignored him in favor of his older acquaintance.

"What brings you to this fair city?"

"To grab some autographs and make an investment."

"I didn't have you pegged as a *Laurel and Hardy* fan."

"George Raft is more my kind of fella."

"I should have guessed."

"How's the wire business, James?"

"So-so. You know how it is. Everybody wants something for nothing and will pay you tomorrow for what you give them today."

"It's the same all around the country. I've set up a lovely situation in Vegas—casinos and other gambling operations in bars and diners."

"Congratulations. We missed you in Los Angeles."

"And this means we feed the bookies under our wing with sports results—I need not explain to you how that works."

"I wish you well. If you want to buy a wire, the Nationwide is second to none."

"Good advertising slogan, James, but as you've mentioned it, Alex and I would like to buy the wire."

"Benny, you didn't need to travel all this way to place an order. A phone call would have been more than sufficient. It's great to see you, but..."

"James, I think you misunderstood. Alex and I want to acquire the Nationwide News."

Benny stared at James Ragen until the man figured out the context of his remarks and then stopped in his tracks, unable to decide whether to take Benny seriously or if it was one of his many jokes of dubious taste and humor.

"Are you kidding with me?"

"No, James, we want to buy the Nationwide. I mean, a stake in it. We have no desire to lose you or your energy, but the growth of your business and our plans for gaming across the country have an alignment of interests. So we are asking for a piece of the action."

James lit a cigarette and puffed at half the stick before saying another word, all the while looking Siegel square in the eye and acting as though Alex wasn't in the room.

"Benny, we go way back, don't we?"

"Ten years or more. You were one of the first fellas I met when I headed out west when Prohibition was ending."

"That means I understand you are a serious man and you know the kind of guy I am. Have you ever known me to have a business partner?"

"Not so's I recall."

"Never, Benny. I create, I own, I manage, and I live off the fat of my land. No sharing with anyone, ever, for anything, and I do not intend to start now."

"I would make a generous offer based on future asset value, but you don't sound that interested in hearing my proposition."

"Damn straight."

"Mr. Ragen," Alex interjected, "Forgive me for saying, but I believe you and Benny have got off on the wrong foot here and I'd like to see if I can put you both right."

Ragen smoked some more and seethed.

"The Nationwide is a fabulous business that creates a more than healthy income for you and any family you may have."

"A wife and son, James Junior."

"That it generates for your wife and little James. We only wish to see it grow as an enterprise and to make sure that the venues under our control, now and in the future, are guaranteed to receive the benefit of the sporting information the Nationwide carries."

"And for this you want a stake?"

"How else can we be certain of always being a happy customer who pays the best rate?"

James smiled again.

"Alex, you have waited while Benny and I had our discussion and then you interceded on his behalf. Congratulations. You are a polite man who understands that there is a time to speak and a moment to be silent. You have wasted your breath because you did not seem to listen to what I said. I will have no business partners. Not with you, not with Benny—no one."

"Is that your last word on the subject, James?"

"You can bet your bottom dollar on it, Benny."

"In that case, we shall not waste any more of your time and will bid you a fond farewell. If at any point you change your mind, then my door is always open. Until we meet again, just one last thing…"

"What's that, Benny?"

"Got any good tips for the two thirty at Saratoga tomorrow?"

ON THE TRAIN back to Vegas the following day, Benny laid out his plan B.

"Without the Nationwide, we will need to establish our own wire service. There are several outfits around the country that would be happy to invest in a rival to Ragen, so we shall have the money to create an infrastructure of our own."

"Good to hear. Did you think Ragen would sell to you?"

"No, but it never hurts to ask. If you shove your hand up enough skirts, one woman'll eventually let you sleep with her."

"Well put, Benny. Always a gentleman. Is that why you're such a hit with the dames?"

"Leave my *shlang* out of it."

"I'm messing with you. Who have you got backing our venture?"

"Interests in Detroit, New York, and Boston—most of the syndicate. We'll build up our network of racetracks and sell into the legitimate bookies in Vegas to begin with."

"And then?"

"Mickey will unearth the less legitimate books and we can then roll out the model we create into other cities like LA or San Francisco."

"The places Ragen wants to maintain control over?"

"San Francisco is open territory right now and, yes, giving Ragen a bloody nose on his home turf would be fun—and good for business too."

12

BENNY HARDLY WAITED to step off the train before making arrangements in Los Angeles and New York for the Trans-American Publishing company to forge its way in the world.

"We will incorporate on the west coast because it'll deliver the message to Ragen that he has a fight on his hands, Alex."

"Should we be so open with him? Would it not be wiser to build the service and sneak up on him unannounced?"

"Are you feeling middle-aged because you're sounding like you are? When I attack a guy, I prefer to run straight at him, punch him in the face and kidneys until he is on his knees, and then kick him until he's unconscious on the mat."

"I'd rather poison the fella and not break into a sweat."

"Either way, that's what we will do and, don't worry, meanwhile we shall fund a bunch of guys to be our eyes and ears at the New York tracks. Then we'll move onto Boston and the other locations dotted around the country where they love to run horses ragged for the pleasure of man."

"You do not sound like you approve of the sport, Benny."

"I prefer games where it is you against the world. Clinging to the sides of a huge animal thundering along a narrow path doesn't appeal. The Big Bankroll loved it, but I'd rather play cards or dice. At least you're not bouncing up and down the entire time."

MEYER BREEZED INTO town seven days later. Benny was pleased to see him but seemed annoyed at him for not announcing the visit beforehand. Alex was just happy to see his friend again.

"Been a while, Meyer."

"But wonderful to hear you're enjoying life in Las Vegas."

"The place has been good for me—and Benny has looked after me too. Thank you for smoothing that over for me because I doubt I would have had the chutzpah to go to him myself."

"Don't worry about it. I told you then and I'll repeat it now: many in the syndicate want to see you succeed and I am one of them. What you and Benny have planned here will change the shape of gambling across this fine nation."

"He always said the future was in casinos."

"That he did, but he had a strange way of explaining himself."

"Still does, Meyer. He has a particular style of looking at the world. Spend enough time with him and you get used to it."

"Have you reached that point yet?"

"He still surprises me on occasion, but I understand him better nowadays. Perhaps he's just calmed down a little—he came across as jittery and impatient when he was a younger man. Nowadays, he understands about maintaining a watchful eye on the goal and not to deviate from it."

"Sounds as though he is as inflexible as ever."

"What I meant was that important matters hold his attention much more now. During those Prohibition years, one minute Benny would do a hit, the next he'd be chasing any old tail that passed before his eyes. He's more grounded."

"Is that because he has a steady?"

"There's his wife and kids, but nobody he's involved with at present."

"Nicely put, Alex."

"I have my moments. Do you have any plans for this evening or can I take you to dinner?"

"THIS MIGHT ONLY be Las Vegas, but this is a world-class restaurant, wouldn't you say, Meyer?"

"It is very good. There's no chicken soup on the menu, but this salmon is most pleasant."

"When we open the Last Frontier later this year, I will make certain we ship in some specialties from New York."

"Cheesecake from Lindy's?"

"Not my top priority, but yeah, if I can sort out the logistics…"

"I'm sure the man who brought hooch from Canada and heroin from Palermo ought to be able to get a takeout from a Midtown eatery in Manhattan."

"I'll do my best, Meyer."

"Only a fool would expect anything less from you."

"Too kind."

"And how is time with Benny working out for you?"

"Like I said earlier, all is good."

"Is he the right man to be running the Trans-American?"

"Why yes. What an unusual question."

"Not at all. Who do you think provided the investment capital?"

"I'm looking at him."

Meyer nodded in acknowledgment, admission that he was the prime financier for the syndicate—ever since the Big Bankroll met his untimely demise.

"So let me ask again, Alex. Is my money safe in Benny's hands?"

"Hand on heart, yes. He has a singular vision and an understanding of what we need to do to make it a reality. The *schnook* you remember has gone and a stand-up guy has replaced him."

"I believe you, Alex, but promise me something."

"Whatever you want."

"If at any point you believe this project is going south, tell me immediately. If the wire comes good then you would have an excellent reason to claim a seat at the syndicate top table. Who'd be able to argue against that?"

"Here's hoping."

"Bring in the big fish and you can worry about it then."

"Follow the money and doors will open."

"Right. Talking of cash, I've hired a new bookkeeper."

"And why should I care about an accounts clerk?"

"When it's Sarah, your ex-wife, I thought you might have an interest."

"Is she doing all right?"

"For sure. I figured if someone was to get visibility into my revenue then I should have somebody with an impeccable moral compass who I can trust implicitly."

"And then you chose Sarah."

"Nice joke, Alex. She left *you*, didn't she? So her judgment isn't that clouded."

"Girl done good, despite her time with me."

"You still see your boys?"

"When I get the chance, Meyer."

"Do you mind that Sarah works for me?"

"Not at all. I'm glad she's keeping herself busy now the lads are becoming men. Besides, there's a new woman in my life."

"Where d'you meet her?"

"In the apartment below my parents' when we first came over from the old country. Then we bumped into each other again in El Rancho. Rebecca is performing later at the Opera House next door if you want to hear her sing."

13

MICKEY HAD WORKED hard since he took over running the gaming in the city. Once El Rancho's staff came to their knees, he hit the road and approached the Vegas bars and identified all the guys who made a book behind a beer glass.

Many of the bookies rolled over with ease—the opportunity to receive protection from a friend of Benny Siegel's was an offer very few could refuse. Though, now and again, Mickey met a guy who was less enthusiastic about losing ten percent of his takings for the right to carry on plying the same trade he was doing before he waltzed in and declared the dive bar part of his territory.

Sometimes, Cohen responded with a slap around the chops and the fella figured the odds pretty quick. Other times, he'd find the need to get rough with the guy. On rarer occasions still, the cops would be called and Mickey would plead down the charges and pay a fine to stop the case getting too serious.

"What are you doing spending time in a jail, Mickey?"

"Who's been snitching to you about my affairs?"

"Relax, my friend. Nobody has been talking out of turn, but if you're going to beat on a guy so bad that he's hospitalized, then make sure there aren't as many witnesses."

Mickey smirked.

"As I was doing it, I told myself, I should drag his sorry ass out into the back alley."

"The least you could have done—placing a call with Ezra or Massimo to lay hands on the guy would have been a better option. That way, no one would see you doing anything and there'd be a separation between you and a bookie bleeding in the street."

"I disagree, Alex. There is nothing like a public kicking to send a simple message to all the scumbags out there who want to argue with me or not hand over their tithe."

Alex knew better than to create an argument with Mickey, but he also felt the fella was causing waves around Vegas, which he could do without lapping at his shore. Mickey might have only been held in a cell overnight, but word was out that he had beaten up a bookie and the guy's life was hanging in the balance at Clark County General. Two bruised ribs and a broken jaw were hardly a sign of imminent death, but that wasn't the point. People believe what they hear, and nobody needed the gaming community to be living in fear. That was bad for business.

"Will you do me a favor, Mickey?"

"What are you after?"

"Next time you pay a visit to a new recruit, do you mind if I tag along? It reminds me of my days in the Bowery."

"If you want to relive your past, be my guest—but don't get in my way."

CLAUD GARFIELD SEATED himself at the end of the bar and men would come up to him now and again for a conversation and a handshake. To the casual observer, Claud was a popular guy, but Mickey and Alex read the situation differently as they sat at a table on the other side of the drinking establishment.

Some of Claud's acquaintances walked straight into the Lucky Pepper, spoke, and left, so the beer was far from the main attraction. Others would mumble to the barkeep before making their way over to Claud. Mickey leaned into Alex for a private conversation.

"He's taking ten, maybe twenty, bets an hour and he isn't paying me a penny for the privilege of working in my town."

"Have you explained to him how the new world is operating?"

"I did as you suggested and let Massimo intercede on my behalf, but when he returned on Friday to collect Garfield's appreciation, he left with bupkis."

With that, Mickey got out of his chair and approached Claud. No rush—a quiet saunter over like he wanted to place a bet. Alex followed him over to the corner spot—Mickey's tone had an edge to it. Having caught up, Alex arrived in time to hear Mickey make his introduction.

"I'm Mickey Cohen—you might have heard of me."

"Your name is familiar, but we've not met."

"A colleague visited you to explain the new situation you find yourself in, but he received no appreciation from you at the end of the week."

"Listen, Mac. This is my patch and I don't pay no one to sit at this bar. Just because you walk in with your dago lackey and your Hebrew charm doesn't mean nothing. You outsiders are all the same to me."

Mickey stepped forward. "Listen to me and listen really carefully. What you do in the Lucky Pepper is your affair, but the minute you take a bet in Vegas it makes it my business and you must compensate me for the right to run a book. I am not asking whether you agree to this—I am telling you how it is."

Claud dropped off his stool and towered over Mickey by a clear eight inches at least, but Alex was still taller.

"I will not pay you a penny. Not now, not ever."

Mickey did a quarter turn to face Alex, smiled, and spoke loudly enough so that most of the bar was in earshot. "Did you hear what Garfield just said to me?"

Claud's attention was focused on Alex who remained silent, looking at Mickey to see what would happen next. He rotated toward Garfield and raised a fist, using the momentum of his twisting to land a jab in the middle of Claud's face. A tooth flew out with the impact and the guy fell backward, caught off his guard, and landed on the floor. Mickey took another pace forward and kneeled down, landing a second punch into Garfield's nose.

The fella tried to shuffle away despite his pain and scurried on all fours toward the restroom twenty feet from the bar. Mickey laughed and remained still to allow his quarry an opportunity to escape—or believe he had a chance to flee. He'd catch up with Claud when the sap arrived at the head door.

Mickey picked him up by the scruff of the neck and threw him into the washrooms. Alex joined them in the tiny space because beating the guy into unconsciousness wouldn't get Mickey his money.

When Alex entered the washroom, Mickey had Claud's head in his hand and he was stuffing it into a toilet bowl, making him drink the water as he gasped for breath.

"That's enough, Mickey."

Alex spoke quietly though with firm conviction, but the hothead either didn't hear or did not want to.

"Stop it, Mickey. We need the guy to agree to make payments to us."

Still no reaction, so Alex placed a hand on Mickey's arm. He swung round with his fist clenched as though he was about to smack Alex in the mouth.

"Keep your nose out of this," he spat. Mickey would end up killing the guy for sure and there had been too many witnesses next door to smooth it over with a thousand-dollar fine and a misdemeanor.

Alex raised both hands, palms facing outward, showing he meant no harm while Mickey remained transfixed. He laid his palms over Mickey's fists until his business partner relaxed his grip. Garfield coughed water out of his lungs and tried to leave the area, but Alex had saved his life for a reason. He grabbed Claud by the collar and hauled him up until he stood on his feet.

"My friend has asked you politely to show him appreciation for allowing you to run a book in this dive. If you enjoy breathing, I advise that you pay ten percent every week whether or not you want to."

Alex eyed Mickey and stared back at Garfield. "Do you agree?" Garfield nodded consent.

"I need you to say it out loud."

"Yes, Mac."

Alex let go and Claud's knees buckled under him and he collapsed onto the floor. With a tap to Mickey's elbow, the two men walked away, leaving Claud to recover from the beating he had just received.

"You shouldn't have done that, Alex. I told you not to become involved."

"Your fists are lethal weapons, Mickey, and I couldn't risk such a valuable commodity as you ending up behind bars just for the sake of a shakedown. I'm not saying the guy didn't deserve to receive a bloody nose. I thought we should get the business transaction out of the way before he lost consciousness."

"Be careful what you do, Alex. I don't like fellas who make me appear foolish."

"I got you your money. Nobody made you look a fool."

Alex exited the bar, worried how Mickey was so quick to temper and the extent to which he seemed out of control as soon as he beat on Garfield.

AUGUST 1942

14

ALEX WAITED A while before making any plans because he wasn't sure he could trust Mickey not to blaze a trail through Las Vegas, beating up bookies like he was trying to fight his way to a championship boxing match. When he thought the former slugger had calmed down enough, he asked Rebecca to go on vacation with him.

"That'd be swell. Where to?"

"Somewhere to guarantee us some sun and the beach."

"Los Angeles?"

"I've spent too much of my life there, already—not that I stayed anywhere near Malibu."

"Cape Cod?"

"Maybe, but I had Florida in mind."

"The Keys. I've never been there."

"Me neither and Miami Beach is supposed to be a great place to stay. Do you fancy a few days alone with me?"

"Sure do. I'll just need to square it with Cashman."

"He won't object—if you remind him I'm the one who'll be whisking you away."

"This will require a whole new wardrobe. I haven't been on a vacation since I was a little girl."

"Here's some clothes money—buy yourself some pretty things and make sure you get a necklace. We can't have a beautiful woman walk around Miami without something sparkling around her neck."

"You're too kind, Alex Cohen."

"You ain't so bad yourself, Rebecca Grunberg."

THEY TOOK THE train to Miami and Alex rented a car under his own name at the station. This was a vacation, and he didn't need to hide his identity from anyone or set himself up with an alibi—an unusual experience for him. She sat in the automobile with a broad grin on her face as they drove over to their hotel on Collins Drive.

"I never thought this would be us in a thousand years."

"What do you mean, Rebecca?"

"When we were kids, did you imagine you'd be driving me around Miami, Florida with enough green in your pocket to never have to work again?"

"Hey, I've done well, but I'm not set to retire any time soon. You're confusing me with some other fella."

"You say that, but I bet you've put sufficient aside over the years to be comfortable for the rest of your life."

"Uncle Sam and my ex-wife took a massive bite into my savings. I gave gelt to Sarah—the Feds swallowed the money from my checking account."

"I didn't mean to open old wounds, Alex… This place is great. Look at the palm trees."

Rebecca pointed at a line of foliage by the roadside, and he glanced at the green fronds as he hit the gas to get them to their hotel before nightfall.

The Hopkins sported a white art deco frontage and a doorman wearing spats—old-fashioned in this day and age. The marble lobby boasted a sweeping staircase which led to a mezzanine floor with a breakfast restaurant, according to the bellboy who began his spiel almost before he'd picked up their bags to take them to their third-story suite overlooking the sea. A five-spot kept the guy smiling as he closed the door on the couple.

Rebecca ran around the suite, brushing her hands against the sumptuous furniture on show in the two bedrooms, living space, and dining room. She marveled at the oil paintings on the wall and the sheer size of the place.

"This must have cost more than a week's wages."

"Don't worry about the price of things. Just enjoy yourself while we're here."

She threw open the balcony doors and stepped outside, flinging herself at the balustrade and staring out at the ocean. "Amazing."

Alex unpacked while Rebecca soaked in the panorama, and then he joined her on the balcony, although he sat on one of the recliners.

"We have this place for the entire week, so the view will still be there after you've hung your things up and got ready for dinner."

"Where shall we go?"

"You tell me. Pick something and I'll get the concierge to organize a booking for us."

"Italian."

"We should be safe with that selection—we are in Miami, after all."

"Huh?"

"Let's just say that many people born close to Mulberry Street live in these parts."

"Is the place crawling with gangsters?"

"No need to be dramatic—but Miami-Dade has a high proportion of casinos and a ridiculously low crime rate."

Rebecca giggled and then froze for a second.

"We are here on vacation, right? You haven't dragged me here to be with your mobster friends?"

"I am here because I want to spend time with you away from Vegas. There is an old friend I would like to visit, but he has been retired for several years. Apart from that, every waking minute will be with you."

"And sleeping minutes too, I hope."

Rebecca's mouth broke into a leering smile and she padded over to sit on his lap. She draped her arms around his neck and they kissed.

TIME FELL AWAY from the couple over the next four nights. They devoted their days to enjoying the beach, the odd foray to stores to buy more trinkets for Rebecca, and hanging in the many coffee shops dotted around town. Every morning, they ate breakfast on the mezzanine or out on the front terrace to watch the world go by while he devoured cereal, scrambled eggs with lox, a bagel with cream cheese and she consumed juice and a slice of toast.

"What should we do today?"

"Hit the beach this morning and the concierge mentioned a place for lunch which could be interesting: Cuban—and I don't even know quite what kind of food that means."

"Sounds like fun. Thank you for all this."

"You can't imagine how much happiness you bring to my life. It is I who should thank you."

She squeezed his palm and he sipped his coffee from the cup in his other hand, emotion welling up inside him.

"Rebecca, this afternoon, why don't you go for a massage?"

"That's a new one. Would there be a female masseuse?"

"This hotel isn't a bordello."

"Will you have one at the same time?"

"No, I need to spend a couple of hours somewhere else."

"On business?"

"Not quite."

"Well? You're making it sound very suspicious—for a man who is meant to be on vacation, remember?"

"There's a fella I used to know who has moved here—I mentioned him when we arrived and I thought I'd swing by and see how he is. You do not have to come. You can but it won't be very interesting for you."

"Who's the guy?"

"Alfonse Capone. You might have heard of him."

REBECCA TOUCHED ALEX'S arm as they sat in their saloon outside a palatial mansion on Palm Island. She had remained by his side for the ten minutes since he'd parked and not left the vehicle.

"Are you all right?"

"Yeah. I was thinking about times gone by and got lost in my past life."

"What happened to Al?"

"Alfonse? He was on top of the world, and then Ness slammed him to the ground for tax evasion. Threw him in jail and left him to die."

"But he's out now."

"Because of ill health. I heard he was beaten up in prison and got his skull smashed—he hasn't been the same since."

They remained in silence as Rebecca mulled that thought over in her head and tried to imagine how bad the beating must have been. The fella was only a name in the headlines to her, but he meant much more to Alex.

"You don't have to come in with me if you'd rather not. I won't mind and he won't know."

"We've been together long enough for me to want to be with you all the time—not just for the shiny moments."

They stepped out of the car and walked up the front path. Almost as Alex rang the bell, the door opened and a guy inquired the purpose of their visit. A brief conversation and the man showed them to a sitting room where they waited only two or three minutes.

Alfonse and Mae Capone appeared and Mae welcomed them to their home and invited them to rest awhile in the shade on the patio by their pool. Alex had spent no time with Mae before—his trips to Chicago had always been on syndicate business and conversation was stilted at the beginning now, but Rebecca helped, drawing the woman into chatting about the weather and their son, Albert.

"He's doing well for himself, isn't he, Alfonse? We're hoping he will graduate and then the world is his oyster."

"Does he come to visit often?"

"When he can. You know how it is with children."

Rebecca looked askance at Mae, whose eyes darted to Alex and back.

"Mae, we don't have any… I mean, we've only been dating a few months."

"Sorry, Rebecca. I knew that Alex had a family and assumed…"

"My family is fine and they live in Hoboken. You weren't to know I got divorced in thirty-six. But you two are going great guns—I admire that longevity in a relationship."

"I supported him during his incarceration."

Without warning, Alfonse stood up from his abject silence and jumped into the pool with his clothes still on. Mae sighed and called for him to swim to the edge of the water. When he eventually followed her command, the butler cocooned him in towels and dried him off. An hour more and Alex thanked Mae for the hospitality and moved to shake Alfonse's hand goodbye, but the man refused, hiding his fingers in his pants pockets.

Alex drove to the Hopkins without uttering a single word, brushing an occasional tear from the corner of his eye. When they got back, he parked in the hotel lot and placed a hand on her leg before she left the car.

"I'm sorry to have put you through that, Rebecca."

"That's all right. He's not how I was expecting."

"Nor me. That was quite a pummeling he got in prison. He used to be so alive—all his faculties firing the entire time."

"Alex, I've seen people like that before and they weren't beaten up. It was the pox."

"Yeah, I figured."

"I understand if you want an early night tonight, Alex."

"No, we've only got three days left so we should squeeze every ounce of life out of our time here. I'll get the concierge to recommend a club—if you fancy trying your hand at dancing without a stage."

"Sounds like heaven."

15

THE SUCCESS OF Trans-American News was hardly remarkable given the amount of effort Alex put into the venture. He pounded the streets of Vegas mopping up every bookie he could find who took bets on any track race in the country. If Trans-American didn't have any eyes on the event when Alex walked in, then by his return a week later, he had the racecourse covered. There were no excuses to refuse his business proposition.

In a short time, Trans-American received payments of a hundred dollars a day from its bookie subscribers. As a director of the company, Alex had a legitimate reason to be rolling in cash. He imagined the advice he'd receive from an accountant like Meyer and stashed most of his extra income into deposit boxes and spent a little on himself and more on Rebecca.

Benny, Mickey and he perched at their usual poolside table at El Rancho and surveyed their world.

"Mickey, you've done well to tie in the bookmakers in Vegas—every single one pays protection to us. And Alex, you've convinced most to buy the wire from Trans-American."

All three smiled at the perfect business they'd built for themselves.

"It's a good start, Benny."

"You never were satisfied, were you, Alex?"

"So everyone else keeps telling me. I just don't want to leave money on the table."

"And what are we missing out on?"

"Vegas has been great for us. We've learned a lot—I know I have—but there are plenty of other cities in this fine country and we should sell Trans-American into those places too."

"Then we'd go head-to-head against James Ragen."

"Depends where we pick next, Mickey. But yes, if he's already got customers, then it's an opportunity for them to choose a different supplier."

"Where do you have in mind, Alex?"

"First, I'd like to go to Los Angeles, because we should hit him on his home turf. If he crumbles there, then other territories will fall in line much easier."

"And if we don't?"

"Then we'll know we've got a fight on our hands and can ramp up the aggravation, Mickey."

"You have all the angles covered, eh?"

"No, Benny. But I have an eye on a huge prize, and I mean to get it."

The three laughed because Alex meant every single one of his bold words and the other two knew it. Convincing illegal bookies to spend money on a wire service when they were already paying through the nose for Ragen's would not be a walk in the park, but nothing worth having ever is.

ALEX TOOK EZRA and Massimo over to LA with him because he needed fellas he could trust and who could handle themselves when trouble came knocking on the door. His lieutenants were all that and more.

A few hours on the train and the men arrived in the City of Angels and settled into a three-bedroom apartment Benny still owned from his days running gaming in the city. It was the perfect cover for a fella to travel round town extorting lowlife degenerate gamblers and their bookmakers.

They spent their first week creating a picture of the city and marked every illegal gambling joint that took bets on horse races. A cross represented a joint with no current wire and a circle was a venue where Ragen already had a client. Then they visited each place on the map they pinned to the living room wall to convert the shape into a square which meant the bookmaker was a confirmed Trans-American customer.

Two months and thirty-six gambling joints later, Alex stared at the picture and surveyed his victories. They started with the crosses because the ones who weren't with Ragen would be easier to turn and all bar two crosses were now a square, showing how successful the three fellas had been since their arrival. The next phase was to take aim at the circles and walk into Ragen territory. Alex looked at the map to decide where they should begin their assault.

ALEX, EZRA, AND Massimo walked into a bar in the heart of Chavez Ravine, the Mexican quarter in the middle of the city. They had to start somewhere and Alex had chosen this spot over all the others because it sounded a tough place to crack.

They ordered a beer each at the bar and hung a while to get the lay of the land. Near the rear of the venue was a guy seated at a table with a stream of short-lived visitors. Alex nudged Massimo and nodded in the general direction. Ezra scratched his neck to give himself an opportunity to view the situation. Having waited as long as his patience would allow, Alex stood up and ambled over to take his position in the informal line of men.

"I'd like to place a bet."

"It's a free country. What's stopping you?"

"No need for the attitude, Mac. Anyone with brains can tell you're the guy to see for these matters."

"Maybe I am, but I don't know you from shit on my shoe."

Alex stared at the bookie for two long seconds and then smiled.

"Forgive me. We haven't been introduced and I have forgotten my manners. My name is Alex Cohen and I would like to place a bet with you on the results of a horse race due to run tomorrow at Saratoga. Do you think you can help me with this request?"

"Señor Cohen, you are in luck because you are speaking to Rodrigo Sanchez and that is what I do for a living."

Both men grinned and the tension eased between them.

"What odds are you giving for fifty dollars on No Hoper at the four o'clock at Saratoga?"

Sanchez blinked and scrunched his face.

"There's no horse running of that name, mister. What do you want?"

"To see if you are as on the ball as I thought you were. Well done."

"What of it?"

"I wish to offer you an opportunity to get better quality track information."

"No deal, bud. I got myself a wire service and that's all I need."

"That is where you and I disagree at the moment, Rodrigo. The thing is I know you use the Nationwide, but that is in the past. From now on, the Trans-American will be your wire of choice."

"And why would I want to switch when I have no need?"

"You're wrong, Rodrigo. You have a pressing need to change because your health will be affected if you stay with the Nationwide."

"Listen, old man. Don't come into my joint and threaten me."

"Would you prefer if we go outside?"

Sanchez stood up and Alex followed him out the side door into an alley—Ezra and Massimo arrived ten seconds later.

The guy took a single glance at the three-against-one odds and cooled his tone before Alex spoke his next words.

"Understand, I don't care what news wire I get, so long as I got one and nobody gets hurt."

"Rodrigo, we want you as a client and not as a corpse—that is bad for business."

"Tell me about it. The thing is that I make my payments to Jack Dragna and he isn't the kind of fella to sit still while you walk around stealing his customers from under him. You speak with him. If he tells me it's okay to buy from you, then I will. If not then our conversation ends here."

Alex took two steps forward so he and Sanchez were only inches apart, pulled out a pistol, and thrust it into the guy's stomach.

"You are stuck in a difficult position, Rodrigo. I feel for you and I have a simple way out. You agree here and now to buy from Trans-American, and I will return my piece to my pocket. If you don't do that, then I shall put a slug in your belly and watch you bleed out before I leave this alley."

Sanchez didn't need more than three seconds to make the decision that saved his life. Even a stranger could tell that Alex meant what he said from the fire in his eyes and the tone of his voice. They settled on an introductory fee and Alex let him go back inside.

"Looks as though we need to pay a visit to Jack Dragna."

LIKE SO MANY bosses before him, Dragna lived in a penthouse suite in a swanky part of town. Alex reminded himself of the feel of marble underfoot as he entered the Brookfield hotel and went up to the reception desk to announce himself.

Up in a private elevator and a gorilla on the top floor frisked him before allowing him into the apartment. Jack Dragna sat at a long wooden table in a red leather chair and beckoned for Alex to sit near him.

"Thank you for taking the time to see me."

"Happy to meet a friend of Benny's."

"Likewise, Jack."

Dragna offered Alex a coffee, which he accepted, but he declined the opportunity to chew on a Danish pastry, although the cinnamon swirl caught his eye more than once during their dialog.

"The primary reason I agreed to this conversation, Alex, was that my men tell me you have been selling your wares in LA and we both know you have omitted to offer me any appreciation for operating in my territory."

"Benny sends his regards and wishes you well. He told me to inform you of his intention to compete with the Nationwide News wire, and Benny understands how you have a lucrative financial arrangement with Ragen to prop him up in Los Angeles."

Dragna stared at Alex and sipped a coffee, occasionally nibbling at a sugary delight on his plate.

"Benny and I have no interest in interrupting your cash flow. All we request is that you support us as we compete with Ragen on our own terms. What does that mean we are asking you to do? Nothing. We are happy to show you our appreciation, and in return, we do not expect you will interfere with our endeavors."

"Alex, let me be clear to you. If you weren't a friend of Benny's, you and your colleagues would be dead by now. In fact, you'd have been killed within days of arriving in my town, but I allowed you to live because of my excellent relationship with Benny Siegel. If you make restitution for not coming to me sooner then we can negotiate in good faith on the matter of the racing wire."

"Let me know what sum you think is appropriate and I will organize the amount to be in your possession before the end of the week, Jack."

Alex didn't begrudge paying a syndicate member a small fraction of his income in LA to keep the business line secure, but why had it taken Jack so long to react to their arrival in town?

April 1943

16

WITH THE LAST Frontier opening in October, Alex offered Rebecca the chance to move to his new hotel and continue her singing career closer to his home, but she refused. While the idea was tempting, as a performer she was happy where she was and he was still welcome to come to any of her shows.

He took that opportunity at least two or three times a week because he loved to watch her perform—just like when they were kids—and that was magnified by the warm glow he felt when the audience applauded at the end of one of her numbers.

Even before the place opened to the public, Alex moved into a cottage in the grounds. It had been designed as a manager's dwelling so had been built to a very high spec.

"If you won't sing on my stage, would you live with me in the Last Frontier?"

He and Rebecca were lying in bed one Saturday morning.

"I'd like to, but I'm not sure. I need my own space. My time with you is great, but there is something healthy about being apart and meeting up again, don't you think?"

"We wouldn't be handcuffed together—you would continue to be the performer you are and I'll carry on with my business interests. The only difference is that we'd share the same living space. I mean, you spend most nights over here, anyway…"

"Let me think about it, Alex. Your suggestion is wonderful and the fact you are prepared to spend so much of your life with me is fabulous. Only…"

"Only you are afraid that this is a slippery slope. One minute you are in my bed, next you're in my house and then you think we'll get hitched and you will be tied to me forever."

Rebecca was silent in response.

"You have nothing to fear on that score—at least not from me. I've been down that road before and I am happy to remain single. I'd be even happier if we were to move in together, but I won't be proposing to you unless you want us to get married, in which case I'll think about it but make no promises."

"Could I have my own room too in the resort? Somewhere I would call my own. I wouldn't spend much time in it, but it'd be there if I needed it."

"Like a security blanket."

"Exactly."

"Sure, why not? The place will not be full to the brim for the first while, anyway."

Alex shrugged in agreement and that settled the matter.

THE FOLLOWING WEEKEND, Alex finished transporting his belongings to the Last Frontier cottage. It was situated five hundred feet away from the main building, surrounded by a small wood and a dozen other cottages, designed as exclusive dwellings for the high rollers at the casino or other elite guests. The manager's residence was the smallest, a mere four bedrooms, with living and dining rooms, as well as a kitchenette, and boasting a veranda that overlooked nothing but a beautiful woodland scene.

Rebecca arrived with her two bags and a painting the next day and put her things in the second bedroom.

"I could use this as a dressing chamber and if we keep the bed here and bring in a table from somewhere, then we wouldn't need to reserve me a room in the hotel. This works great as a private space just for me."

"Are you sure? I've already issued instructions for the front desk to expect you to check in later today."

"It's fine, Alex, but thanks for your understanding."

"You don't want to be cooped up here, trapped with nowhere to go. I think that was Sarah before she walked out on me, and I do not want you to experience the same crap I put her through."

"You're a better man than that, Alex."

"Don't be so certain. I've had several life-changing moments and not one of them has been pleasant—apart from the births of my sons."

"Not for Sarah, I bet." He grimaced and nodded—childbirth was no laugh.

The couple found a new balance with Alex popping over to El Rancho to watch Rebecca sing and dance, his mind almost always harking back to those halcyon days when the most he hoped for was the sight of an ankle beneath a swirling skirt. In the intervening years, the woman had altered her attitude to revealing more than just a thigh.

THREE SATURDAYS ON and Alex went straight to the cottage after catching Rebecca's first show of the night. He didn't have the energy for the midnight performance—it had been a long week and he needed some rest. At two in the morning, the front door burst open and Rebecca stood there, clinging to the jamb, sobbing.

Alex woke in an instant and ran to her, but she wouldn't let him touch her. Instead, she staggered and collapsed onto a couch, still crying her lungs out.

"What's happened?"

The tears only lasted for five minutes, by which time Rebecca had calmed down enough to utter a handful of words.

"He put his hand up my dress."

"Who?"

"I pushed him away, but he wouldn't stop."

"Which guy? Where?"

"He dragged me to his room."

"One of the guests?"

"Tore my robe."

"Which guest?"

"Huh?"

"How did you get away?"

More sobs, and then they abated.

"He had me sit on the bed. When he stood up to take his pants down, I punched him in the balls and ran out the room."

Rebecca loosened her folded arms for the first time since her arrival in the cottage. The front of her blue satin dress was torn from top to toe and was only held by a thread at the bottom hem.

"I want to be sure you are okay. Did he… do anything else?"

"No. If I'd stayed there for more than a few seconds, then he'd have done far worse than a hand on my leg."

"Tell me who did this, Rebecca."

"I can't."

"If you didn't catch his name, we will figure out which room he took you in."

"Can I have a shot of vodka?"

Alex strode into the kitchen, found a bottle, and poured two glasses. She gulped hers down in a single swallow.

"I know which room and I know who did this, but I cannot tell you the name."

"Why?"

Rebecca stood up and walked into their bedroom to return a moment later in a housecoat. The trail of her blue dress lay on the floor.

"If I give up the name, then you'll do something about it—I cannot allow you to do that on my behalf. You will be sweet and protective of me to want to take action, but it is not your fight. It is mine."

"Why would you not want me to act?"

"Have a think for a minute, Alex, and answer the question for yourself."

Alex pondered for a short while, and then he understood.

"It was Benny."

Rebecca looked down and nodded, a shudder rippling through her body. Alex's hand formed a fist and he bit into the knuckle. Siegel was a renowned womanizer despite having brought his wife and kids out to Los Angeles, and then Vegas, with him. The stories of his conquests were varied and many—entertaining anecdotes when the men were sharing a drink. Until now.

"He is my boss, your business partner and ally. What happened to me shouldn't change your relationship with him. It'd cost you too much."

"That's not what's important, Rebecca."

"I'll deal with Siegel in my way. I don't need you to fight my battles."

"When a friend behaves badly, his friends should call him on it. Do you think I can ignore what he has done to you?"

"You must."

"Right now, I want to go to his room and shoot him in the…"

"And that is why you can't take any action. If you work with Benny, then you'll return to the syndicate. Whacking him is not the way to win friends back home."

"So, Rebecca, you want me to sit on my hands?"

"Don't make this about you, Alex. Benny assaulted me and I am the one who will deal with the *verstinkener momzer* in my way and in my own sweet time."

17

ALMOST EVERY SMALL-time bookmaker in Las Vegas paid for the opportunity to get the Trans-American wire and avoid being on the receiving end of an arson attack. But there was one lone voice of dissent and it came from a large establishment, which meant Alex needed to take them under his wing as soon as possible. The longer they didn't pay their dues, the greater the chance that the other bookies might dispense with his services.

Gavin Wolff operated out of the back of a bar on Fremont called The Red Pheasant. As a drinking venue, it was pleasant but nothing fancy. People popped in for a beer, but they stayed for the betting. Alex brought his lieutenants to check out the joint.

There were four cashiers in a row receiving the wagers, and behind them was a huge blackboard stretching the entire wall. Scurrying along with stepladders on wheels were three guys writing and rewriting the odds on every race taking place across America that afternoon.

"This is quite an operation they've got here."

"And some, Ezra. Either of you two spotted Wolff?"

His men shook their heads and the three continued to watch the room. While his lieutenants concentrated on the people, Alex's eyes were drawn to the cables attached to the wall and skirting.

At the far end of the cashiers was a fifth man, whose ear was glued to a telephone receiver while he scribbled onto a notepad. Each time he finished another scrap of paper, he threw it behind him and a boy picked it up and distributed it to the three guys on ladders.

The cable coming out of the phone stretched to the wall ran on top of the blackboard and out into the back. The power in this room lay in the racing wire, and that was why Wolff couldn't be seen. This guy wasn't taking bets, he was running the joint from behind closed doors.

Alex nudged Ezra and the two lieutenants joined him as he walked over to the door which was shut and had a gorilla with no neck to prevent unwanted guests being foolish enough to wander in without permission.

"You got two options right now. Let Wolff know he has visitors or don't. Either way, we are going in and *you* are not stopping us."

Alex stressed his point by digging what felt like the barrel of a gun into the fella's belly and he went inside to announce their arrival. The three pushed past the gorilla and stood in Wolff's office while the man himself sat at a large oak desk, in front of which were a handful of chairs—a long couch, armchair, and coffee table were ten feet away but nobody looked as though they would get comfortable and chat.

"Freddie tells me you do not have an appointment and that you were insistent that you should see me anyway. For what do I earn this approbation?"

"I want to offer you a business proposition and I believe you will find it so compelling we shall sign a contract before my associates and I leave this room."

Wolff put his feet up on his desk, leaned back in his chair, and chuckled.

"You have this place confused with somewhere else. This isn't backstage at some theater show, even though you are acting like some comedian. Get out of here before Freddie causes you some discomfort."

Alex nodded at Massimo, who grabbed the hapless Freddie by the throat and pinned him to the wall, raising his arm slightly so that Freddie's feet barely touched the ground. Within seconds, choking noises emanated from his larynx. Alex turned to face Wolff.

"Now that we have got the pleasantries out of the way, why don't we introduce ourselves. I am Alex Cohen and you are Gavin Wolff."

The guy let both feet drop off the desk to the ground and he let out a whistle, pushing his Stetson to the back of his head.

"I did not realize who you were."

"No matter. If Massimo releases his stranglehold on Freddie, can we assume that the chump will leave us in peace?"

"His only job is to prevent riffraff from entering my inner sanctum."

Alex issued another nod and Freddie scurried out of the room to let the adults talk. After the door was shut, Alex perched on the couch, forcing Wolff to walk out from behind his desk and sit on the easy chair nearby. Massimo maintained his position near the exit and Ezra sat next to his boss.

"You are a busy man and I do not wish to waste your time. The business proposition is simple and I hope you find it amenable. I want you to cease your contract with the Nationwide and subscribe to the Trans-American wire instead."

"The Nationwide covers more tracks and their service has worked fine for me from the start. My margins are at least ten to twenty percent fatter thanks to James Ragen. I do not need to leave him."

"Gavin, we are both men of the world and understand how business is conducted. Sometimes it is not the quality of the service that dictates who beats the competition, but the overall package on offer. You are correct that the Nationwide has marginally greater coverage, although we will narrow that gap within the next six months."

"You see—"

Alex raised a finger to halt Wolff.

"And it is the package on offer that you should focus on and not the details of which tracks we can offer a results facility today."

"What package? You're selling a news wire."

"Ragen sells a racetrack news service. I sell racing news and insurance cover."

"Why put those together?"

"Gavin, they are inseparable. How can you be certain you are calculating the best odds if a corner of your mind is worrying whether your place of business is mysteriously going to be subjected to an arson attack?"

"Mr. Cohen, I have no such concerns. My competition is small fry and won't assault my premises. They are more likely to do something dumb like undercut my odds until they can't make any money."

"Gavin, you are wrong. In fact, word on the street is that this bar will go up in flames tonight."

Alex sniffed the air for smoke so much that Wolff looked around and inhaled himself. Then he stopped himself—much to Ezra's amusement.

"If you buy from the Trans-American, then your subscription includes an insurance against such events occurring. More than that, you receive my personal guarantee that your business will be trouble free from this moment on."

Alex waved a hand in the air and Ezra revealed a bunch of papers he had stuffed inside his jacket pocket.

"The contract is here and all you need to do is put a signature on it."

"Mr. Cohen—Alex—forgive me, but I cannot sign paperwork unseen and unchecked by my lawyer, even if the terms are first class."

Another wave and Ezra procured a pen and placed it on top of the papers on the table next to Wolff. Alex stared at the man, waiting.

"I want you to understand something, Gavin. Unless I have your signature on that contract before I leave this room, then you had better pray the fire service can get over here in good time before you lose your livelihood."

"You're threatening me."

"I am advising you of the consequences of your actions. Nothing more. I hope to help you reach a sensible commercial decision. Your bookmaking operation might be expendable, but my reputation is not, Mr. Wolff. I mean what I say and have given you fair warning—choose between this contract or a pile of ashes. I would prefer us to become business partners, but if that is not possible then you will have no business. Those are your options, and you must make a choice now."

"This is daylight robbery."

"I am not stealing from you—we are exchanging money for a service. Please do not utter libelous statements about me. I do not appreciate those who tarnish my reputation. Will you sign?"

Alex pushed the contract three inches nearer to Wolff, who looked at the front page and licked his lips. Five, ten, fifteen seconds and he picked up the pen, opened the document, and signed in all the right places.

"An excellent decision, Gavin. Thank you for being our latest customer. You won't regret this. My people will be around tomorrow to help you move over to Trans-American News."

Wolff stood up and shook Alex's hand—still on autopilot—he couldn't believe he'd been forced to buy a wire service without even finding out how much it would cost. As Alex and his associates walked out of the room, Wolff reminded himself that he still had his health and the place would not burn down any time soon.

18

BENNY WASN'T THE only fella who had difficulties keeping it in his pants. Alex hadn't spoken with Mickey in almost a week which was unusual. He enjoyed talking about the old days and reminiscing about times in Chicago and New York—places and people they both shared from their past. Alex didn't mind chatting over times gone by, but having seen Alfonse only recently, memories of the Windy City held less of a luster for him nowadays.

"You know where Mickey is holed up?"

"No, boss. Haven't seen him for ages."

"Massimo, tell me if you hear anything from him."

A day traveling from one bookmaker to the next delivered more sightings than Alex and his men could possibly track down, as so many of them had him in two places at once. That evening the three sat in the Last Frontier bar to figure out a plan.

"Are there any bookies or bars we haven't visited?"

"Not that I know of, Ezra—but the fella can't have vanished. And if he has to be somewhere, then it is our job to find him."

"There is always the possibility that he's buried out in the desert."

"Massimo, you're right and although Mickey has a brusque manner, I am unaware of anyone who would bump him off— assuming we ignore any disgruntled bookie who thought the subscription rates to Trans-American were too high."

"When we looked into the whites of their eyes this week, we'd have noticed if someone wasn't kosher."

"I agree, which means we have been looking in the wrong places. If Mickey's not in a bar or a bookmaker's, where would he be?"

"Brothel."

Massimo and Ezra gave the answer at the same time and smiled at each other in acknowledgment. Alex nodded.

"Looks like we'll have to wear out more shoe leather on the fella. At least, let's think smart. Use your crews to search all the nafkas we run in Vegas and we'll see if we can get a lead before we are forced to go into every bedroom and check under the mattress."

JUST BEFORE ALEX settled down for lunch the following day, he received a message from the desk clerk at the Frontier. Ezra had found Mickey, who had been resting in the same boudoir from the moment he first disappeared. Alex figured the chances were that he would remain in the same location for another hour while he went to the restaurant to grab his food before meeting Ezra in the lobby and heading out.

They drove past El Rancho and continued north for half a mile until they reached a building on the edge of town. As with many of the most vibrant places in the city, it didn't look like much from the outside. Although this bordello was owned by Alex, he hadn't imagined this was where Mickey might have gone. Lois greeted the men and started her spiel but halted in her tracks when she recognized Alex and Ezra.

"You here on business or pleasure, gentlemen?"

"Work, Lois. Ezra's heard there's a john in one of your rooms who has been here for best part of a week. That true?"

Lois sighed because her gravy train was about to go off the rails.

"Yeah. He's on the second floor—at the far end."

"You know who he is?"

"If I didn't when he walked in, he sure made certain we all learned within a minute of his arrival."

"But no call to inform either of us that our mutual friend had his pants around his ankles as a room guest?"

"I'm not being funny, Alex, but I didn't think you'd want me to bother you every time one of your fellas turned up to have a private party."

"Good point, Lois–although you might consider it was worth dropping a dime after the second entire day, though?"

"Uh-huh. To be honest, we've earned more from him than from the rest of the rooms put together this week, and we were hoping the party would last forever."

"They never do, Lois. You should know that."

She nodded and shrugged because Alex was right—a phone call was the least Lois owed him.

"Anybody with him now, or is he resting?"

"He's paid us for a full day's company in advance and he handed over more dough just before lunch. So if he is awake or asleep, then there's a girl in the room with him—it's what he's paying for."

"Will you take me to him now, please, Lois?"

SHE OPENED THE door and Alex stepped in. Ezra made to follow him, but Alex asked him to remain outside.

"If you hear any ruckus, then come in, but let's try to leave Mickey as much of his dignity as remains."

Ezra dragged a chair from further down the corridor and settled in and waited–this was a job that would not be hurried.

The interior wallpaper comprised red stripes, and the swirls in the carpeting hid a multitude of stains. Alex surveyed the scene of Mickey flat on his back on the bed with the nafka sat at her dressing table sneaking glances at a book on her lap. She turned her head as Alex entered the room but registered nothing more of his presence. He walked over and took her novel, flipped a look at the front cover, and returned it.

Alex placed a single finger over his lips to show the girl should remain silent and when she acknowledged that instruction, he pointed at the corridor and indicated she should walk over there and vamoose. As she closed the door behind her, Mickey snored so loudly Alex believed he saw the walls shaking. The noise was disturbing enough to wake Mickey from his slumber, and he blinked twice until he found his bearings. Then he sat up and searched the bedside table for a smoke.

"Where's Bernice?"

"Went out for a breather. She couldn't keep up with you."

"Figures. None of them broads got the stamina to spend much time with Mickey Cohen."

"That so?" Alex looked around and threw Mickey's shorts on his lap. "You must be the only john in the world who's paid for the day and not the hour. I admire your prowess—if that's the right word."

"Sounds mighty fine to me."

Alex popped his head out the door and asked Ezra to hustle up a pot of coffee. Five minutes of listening to Mickey's boasting and Bernice came in with a tray containing the drink and a pile of sandwiches. Alex gave her a hefty tip.

He poured two mugs and offered one to Mickey, who seemed more interested in locating some vodka he'd mislaid from earlier. Alex picked up an empty liquor bottle peeking out from under the bed.

"This what you're looking for?"

"Yep. Anything left inside her?"

"Only your own spit, Mickey. Have a coffee instead."

"Don't want to. Wanna bottle of hooch and Bernice sat on top of me."

"Mickey, you've had enough fun to last most men a lifetime. I need you to sober up, take a shower, and come back to work. Why d'you go on this bender, anyway?"

Mickey eyed him cautiously, the way only a drunk can—his head swaying because his balance was shot to hell. Mickey's eyes weren't working well enough to let him focus on Alex, as his neck refused to stay still.

"None of your goddamn business, Alex. Bring Bernice to me, and perhaps I'll tell you all about it."

"No dice. Coffee and a shower—that's what you're getting. You won't be seeing Bernice for a while. There's a gaming operation you are supposed to be running."

"Leave me alone, Alex. You're not my boss. You seem to forget that you used to be somebody, but nowadays you are nothing—just one of Benny's crew. And that means you can't go ordering me about. I do what I want and it is none of your business."

Alex remained seated and had no desire to argue with a drunk Mickey. He smelled the guy's verstinkener breath from the other side of the room.

"I've been very patient with you, Mickey, but that is wearing thin now. You have been out of action for an entire week and it would appear that all you have achieved is to empty the bar downstairs and give Bernice a chance to finish *War and Peace*."

"Huh?"

"Never mind. Take a shower and get to work. I will be on the first floor finishing my coffee. If you are not down in thirty minutes, I'll hop over to El Rancho and inform Benny that his right-hand man is banging his girls."

Mickey rolled off the bed and staggered over. He drew back a fist. "Don't you tell me what to do. You are no better than me. If you give me one more order, so help me I'll punch your lights out."

Alex stood up and headed for the door. Just before he closed it behind himself, he turned and said, "Thirty minutes, Mickey."

19

BENNY SIEGEL CONTINUED to maintain a hand in some gaming operations in Los Angeles. Without Guy McAfee to look after business there, he was drawn to take matters into his own hands now and again.

Most of the time this was just the way of the world, but occasional difficulties would ensue and the cops would arrest him on a variety of charges. Then he would appear in court, express his sincerest apologies for his misdeeds and, with the help of a generous donation to the judge's benevolent fund, would pay a fine and move on in his life.

For Benny, it was the price of doing business, but he did not appreciate the attention he received from the newspapermen and the nickname they gave him. He did his best to leave it alone and Alex advised him not to respond in public, even though Mickey told Benny to smack any guy in the kisser who called him Bugsy.

"Alex, they made up the phrase because in the last court case, a bookie said I had acted all crazy—bugged out—but I'm never too sure they're not talking about my eyes."

He looked at Benny and didn't quite get what he meant, and then he stared again by squinting at him and understood why he was so sensitive. In the half-light, his eyeballs appeared to push out from his face, but in all the years Alex had known Benny, he had noticed nothing about them before. Alex could write a long litany of the problems he had with Siegel, but the fella's eyes were not on the list.

ONE EVENING ALEX and Benny met up after dinner. Rebecca was performing in the late show at the Last Frontier, having left El Rancho several months before, so Alex planned on catching up with Benny and then hoofing it back to the Frontier to catch Rebecca's act around midnight.

At the El Rancho bar, Benny had hit the sauce early, judging by the extent to which he was slurring his words when Alex arrived at nine. The chances of business getting discussed reduced to zero by the time he heard him speak.

"Did you see the sheets today? My name is all over the papers—in LA and here too. It's like the press wants to hound me to death."

"The one thing I've learned about them newspaper boys is that it is never personal and always about what sells their stories. My picture was on the front page of every New York news rag for weeks —or at least that's how it felt to me. Truth was that I had three days of notoriety and a month of people squinting at me as they tried to figure out where they'd seen my face before. It all passes over."

"Might be true for you, but not for me, Alex. The trial they've dredged up again took place last year, and still they're going on about it."

"Is there an election soon? Candidates like to sound strong on law and order—you and I are the people they'll name because johns have a perception of what we do and how we behave."

"Just businessmen, right?"

As Benny finished speaking, he raised a solitary finger and the waiter appeared—he ordered a vodka martini, straight up with a slice, and Alex asked for a Scotch on the rocks. While this was happening, Alex picked up Benny's newspaper and read above the fold.

The article was a rehash of Benny's trial with the added twist that a cop was on the take and had been in the same bar as Benny at some point in the past when Siegel lived in LA. The whole piece was tenuous and just a feeble excuse to slap Benny's photo on the front page to make a few more sales. The johns liked to read about their hotel owners and the families who owned most of the land in Vegas, and gained pleasure in hearing about the downfalls of the recent arrivals in the neighborhood, especially if they were Jewish.

Benny forgot about sipping martinis and emptied his glass before Alex tasted his liquor. The waiter delivered another cocktail in short order.

On the other side of the pool, a group of four nudged elbows and pointing in their vicinity. Were he and Benny making a scene or had the foursome recognized the syndicate members?

The two couples meandered toward the men, and Alex monitored their journey while he listened to Benny complain about the state of the nation's press.

"Hey, we think you're famous. Are you, bud?"

They aimed the question at Benny, but the way the guy swaggered, Alex could have been forgiven for thinking the inquiry was aimed at him. Benny ignored the kid, as he was so wrapped up in his own misery.

"Mac, I'm talking t' ya. You famous or something?"

Benny raised his head and glanced at the guy.

"What's your name, son?"

"Hal Bishop."

"Listen to me, Hal. I am not famous, but you might have seen me around. Now go back to your table with your friends and leave me the hell alone."

Hal's smile dropped from his face and he scowled as he took in the instruction. Then his eyes widened when he saw the newspaper next to Alex.

"You're Bugsy Siegel."

Benny leaped out of his chair and pounced on Hal. Before the guy knew what was happening, Siegel pushed him to the ground and kicked him in the kidneys. Alex attempted to pull his friend off the tourist, but Benny was in no mood to be dragged anywhere. The two women in the group screamed and a huddle of waiters surrounded the melee. Meanwhile, the steel toe of Benny's shoe made contact with Hal's stomach and head three times.

Alex got a better purchase on Benny's arms and hauled him five feet away—far enough for his legs to no longer be able to kick his hapless opponent.

"Everyone, calm down. You too, Benny."

Alex shot a glance at the nearest waiter. "Give everybody here a drink on the house as we have disrupted their evening."

Then he continued to hold onto Benny, who he felt was trying to slip from his clutches to begin the second round. Hal remained on the floor and his woman cradled his bleeding head. The other two stood there like chopped liver.

"Why don't we move this disagreement outside?"

"You need to call the cops. That guy can't go around beating on people." Hal's girlfriend had a point, but now was not the time for an argument.

"Tell you what. Let's all go out to the lobby and take things from there. Are you able to stand, Hal?"

Bishop nodded and fumbled his way to his feet, assisted by his friends. The six exited the restaurant and meandered over to reception—all the while, Alex kept pace with Benny, who was still seething and was in no mood to discuss anything.

Near the entrance, the waiters had called ahead and the concierge, along with two security guards, were waiting for the group. Alex indicated for them to hang back because his plan was to diffuse the scene as much as possible as tempers were running high and more hotel staff would only inflame the situation.

"I understand this has put a crimp in your day, but I also hope you appreciate that Mr. Siegel has a right to privacy."

"Look what he did to Hal." The girlfriend sobbed and the other couple shuffled nervously. They had gone out for an evening's fun and the night had turned sour. As they had read the papers, they knew that Benny was a gangster and that made them very nervous.

"We should go, if that's all right with you, Hal?"

Bishop nodded and spat more blood onto the floor. Alex couldn't tell if the guy was aiming for their shoes or just trying to clear the gunk from his mouth.

"Benny, if you don't mind, I think we should offer Mr. Bishop some form of compensation for the evening's misadventure. Would you be willing to discuss the size of this consideration, Mr. Bishop?"

"You mean money?"

"Why yes? You have been inconvenienced and should receive something to acknowledge it. In return, we would like this matter to stay among ourselves. There would be no need to involve the local police."

Alex's eyes bored into Hal's, gauging how likely he was to take a few shekels for his silence. Benny understood what Alex was doing and stopped seething for a short while.

Hal wrestled his elbow from his friend's grip and found he could stand by himself, despite the blood and bruises to his torso.

"I would be happy to come to an arrangement. How much are we talking?"

"Hal, why don't we hop into Mr. Siegel's office to iron out the details? We'll all be more comfortable there."

Hal's girlfriend interjected. "I think I'll go home now, dear. This whole situation has left me feeling queer. Will you be all right without me?"

"Sure, but this'll only take a minute. You could rest here while we men talk business."

"Could you call me a taxi instead? This has all been too much."

Even if Hal couldn't figure out what was happening, Alex sure did. The girl had no appetite to spend time with Hal any more this evening because he looked wretched and bloody—and would just need tending to.

She wasn't married to him and felt no desire to act like his mother. She was with Hal to have fun and nothing more. Meanwhile, Hal had dollar signs coming out of his eyes and had forgotten he had taken this woman out for an evening to show her a good time. Alex nodded at the concierge, who organized a cab within a minute. The girl pecked her boyfriend on the cheek and was gone. Alex, Hal, and Benny walked into his office and they all sat down.

"How about five hundred dollars and we call it quits?"

"The trouble is, Mr. Siegel, that you hurt me and I might need medical attention. I don't know if that will be enough to cover my expenses."

"Then a thousand should provide for a hospital bill and still leave you plenty to buy a fabulous meal for you and your girl."

Hal thought for a second and held out his hand to shake on the agreement. Benny sealed the deal and got Hal to sign a sheet of paper that said this was full and final settlement of the matter. Alex and Benny knew it wouldn't stand up in court, but Hal was happy enough—especially when Benny produced the gelt out of a petty cash box.

"Let me walk you to your car to show there's no hard feelings."

Alex went with them as far as the lobby and watched the two men leave the hotel. When they were three hundred feet ahead, he wandered outside until he caught up with them, as they stopped at a vehicle that Hal unlocked. A brief flash erupted from nowhere in the dark and a split second later, a bang of the revolver. Hal had learned the hard way that nobody ever used the name Bugsy around Benny and lived to tell the tale.

December 1943

20

"I THINK YOU'LL want to come over and pay me a visit."

Alex listened on the line and tried to decide whether Jackson Garnett was on the level. It was the first night of Hanukkah, the Jewish festival and while he was disinterested in such things, Rebecca still enjoyed the traditions of her childhood and wanted him home in time to light some candles, say a prayer and exchange a small gift.

"For real?"

"I wouldn't bother you if this didn't matter—you'll understand when you get here."

He warned Ezra and Massimo to stick near a phone in case he needed the cavalry and headed out to Garnett's office a few miles down the road, south of the Last Frontier. When he walked in, Jackson was nowhere to be seen and the desk sergeant acted like it was his life's goal to be the biggest pain in the ass in the world.

"What business do you have with Sheriff Garnett?"

"He knows why I am here."

"That may be so, but until you tell me, I can't allow you to pass to the other side of that gate."

The cop indicated a small wooden swing door which separated the desks from the waiting area.

"In that case, I'll wait for Jackson to show. If he's in the joint, let him know that Alex is here."

Fifteen long minutes later and Garnett appeared from a doorway that led to the cells. He smiled when he saw Alex and walked over—his weekly extra paycheck might prove a useful investment this early evening.

"Thanks for popping over. You should have told Bill to get me instead of hanging around here and waiting."

"Sergeant Bill thought he wanted to know my business and even though I explained to him to keep his nose out of my affairs, he insisted on doing nothing without everything typed in triplicate."

Jackson glared at Bill who was oblivious to the offense he had caused, but Alex knew that hick cops didn't understand city ways and ignored the flatfoot.

"Let's forget about old Bill and deal with the matter at hand. Will you come into my office?"

Jackson led Alex through the little gate, past the desks and their typewriters, and into his room with a frosted glass door. He invited Alex to sit down and offered him a coffee.

"Tell me what was so damn important that I had to get into my car and drive over here?"

"Before we start, I want you to know that I had no part in this happening."

"What has happened that's nothing to do with you?"

"We've got a fella in the cells downstairs."

Alex blinked twice, but Jackson seemed to think he'd given enough of an explanation.

"Who is this mystery felon?"

Jackson looked quizzically back.

"I thought you knew—we arrested Mickey Cohen two hours ago."

"WHAT THE HELL happened, Mickey?"

Alex had demanded to see Mickey immediately, and Jackson hustled him down the stairs. When they reached the cells, Alex soon spotted Mickey because the others were just kids caught making mischief.

"I got pulled over by some greenhorn who didn't recognize who I was and the next thing I knew, he had me eating the paint of my car hood and had slipped cuffs on me."

Alex let Mickey continue his tirade of complaints for a while until he couldn't take it any more.

"Why did the cop stop you in the first place?"

"He reckoned I was weaving over the road."

"Did he have just cause?"

"I don't know, Alex. I can't remember, but the gumshoe had no reason to use handcuffs."

"Did you threaten him or act in any way that he might construe you intended him any harm?"

"You joking with me? When he asked to see my license, I passed him my wallet and left an appreciation for him. That's when he hauled me out of my vehicle and ran me in."

"You know what the charges are?"

"They haven't told me zip since I got here. The cop processed me, Garnett showed up, and the guy threw me into this cell and I've heard bupkis after that."

Alex surveyed the scene as the three young men in the adjoining cell craned to hear Mickey's whispering. He might have been angry, but he was no fool.

"Let me talk to Jackson and figure out how we can straighten this out. I'll get you a coffee or something."

"I don't need a coffee—I need to be free."

"One step at a time, Mickey. And no disrespect, but you stink of booze and need a hot drink."

BACK IN GARNETT'S office, Alex sat down opposite his host and sighed.

"Mickey said your flatfoot processed him. What happened?"

"Denzel Waterman followed Mickey for over a mile as he was swerving all over the place. When the officer stopped him, Mickey was verbally abusive and tried to bribe him. At that point, Waterman asked him to leave his vehicle and Mickey refused. Then he cuffed him and brought him in."

"How long has Waterman been in the squad?"

"It's his first week—his first collar, actually."

"Where were you when Waterman arrived here with Mickey?"

"Out dealing with a domestic dispute. By the time I returned, Waterman had fingerprinted Mickey and was typing up the paperwork to book him. That's when I figured the best thing to do was get Mickey in a cell and to call you before this got more out of hand."

"You said it. What made Waterman feel the need to create a file before interviewing Mickey?"

"Your friend was so far gone that Denzel thought it was an open and shut case."

"Have you had a word with the greenhorn and explained who Mickey is?"

"I didn't have to. Even old Bill knew Mickey as soon as he walked in and tried to convince Waterman to play it quietly, but Denzel was psyched up with his first ticket and refused to listen to reason."

"Where is the boy now?"

"At his desk. I told him to check everything he'd typed up and suggested first drafts of forms can find themselves in the trash sometimes."

"And do you have a good answer why that wizened old crow of a sergeant didn't intervene and stop Waterman in his tracks? I mean, they fingerprinted Mickey. Where's that record sheet?"

Jackson waved a piece of yellow paper from his desk and Alex beckoned for it to be handed over. Garnett followed the instruction and Alex tore the card into fingernail-sized pieces, emptied the trash on the floor, threw the bits into the receptacle, and tossed in a lit match. Then he took a second one to light his cigarette.

"What do you want me to do now, Alex?"

"Bring in Waterman."

"Would it better if I deal with him so he doesn't see... our relationship?"

Alex pondered for a moment and agreed.

"Make sure Waterman understands this is his only mistake with me. The next time he arrests one of mine, he must explain his actions to me directly."

"I understand and I appreciate how you're handling this. It's mighty big of you."

"And have a word with Bill—he might have known Mickey, but he did not show me any respect when I walked in today and that has incurred my displeasure."

"I'll see to it, Alex. Nobody intended any disrespect."

Alex raised an eyebrow but let the comment go. Bill knew better than to poke his nose where it didn't belong, even if the rookie had blundered into a dangerous situation of his own making.

IN THE CAR, Mickey and Alex sat having a smoke before they headed back to where Mickey had been forced to abandon his vehicle.

"I will pay a visit to Officer Waterman's home when he goes off his shift."

"And, Mickey, what will you do then?"

"Put a bullet through his brains and bury him in the desert with all the other scum."

"Let's not get ahead of ourselves. The guy made an honest mistake in refusing to take your money, but he doesn't deserve to meet his maker for being too upright a citizen."

"Alex, that's where you are wrong, but then you weren't the one handcuffed in the back of a traffic car."

"Mickey, you were driving under the influence. This never would have happened if they'd had the good sense to keep the Volstead Act."

Mickey's expression showed he thought Alex's whimsy was misplaced.

"Alex, don't get high and mighty with me. The kid disrespected me and he needs to be taught a lesson."

"That may be so, but death is not what you should be teaching. I've had a word with Garnett and Waterman will soon see the error of his ways."

"Eye for an eye, Alex."

"If that is true then as you are not dead, there is no need for him to be whacked. You have been waylaid for two hours and he will spend at least a month stuck in the station house doing filing for the squad. You'll get your retribution."

"I still think he deserves a shallow grave."

"Let's return you to your car and we can decide then. Just remember that we do not need any heat from a cop-killing haunting us right now. Bill saw you in his cells and if Waterman is hit, even an old-timer desk sergeant will want to know whether you had an alibi."

"I guess—but I don't like it."

"Who does, Mickey?"

February 1944

21

VALENTINE'S DAY HAD a special place in Alex's heart ever since he traveled to Chicago and assassinated seven members of the North Side Gang in a botched attempt at killing Alfonse's enemy, George Moran. That was 1929, and this was now—Rebecca had a different relationship to February 14.

Having spent so many years on the road and alone, she got a real buzz out of the day. She left a brief note in Alex's pants pocket and gave him a card almost as soon as he woke up.

"You must wait until later for your present."

"Rebecca, there is no need to buy me something. Being with you gives me all the pleasure a man could want."

"Does that mean you haven't bothered getting me anything?"

She scrunched up her nose and put her hands on her hips, as though admonishing him. But they both knew better than that. Besides, whenever Alex noticed any pretty trinket, he'd buy it just because it was there. Rebecca was not lacking in gifts from her man.

When he got home that night to get ready for their evening together, she had sprinkled rose petals in a path from the hallway of the cottage. A muffled voice asked, "Is that you?" and Alex answered in the affirmative. "Wait a second and come on through."

He counted ten elephants and sauntered along the steady stream of petals, through the living room and into their bedroom. And there she was—the most beautiful woman in the world, kneeling on the bed, wearing only a giant red ribbon across her chest tied in an enormous bow and not a scrap of clothing more.

"Don't you want to open your present now, Alex?"

HE HAD FOUND a chi-chi restaurant at the edge of town—a family-run place with an Italian menu and a solid reputation for its desserts. Although he had only phoned the joint a week before, they could, of course, accommodate his booking on this special day—which was his way of life in Vegas nowadays.

He drove them over and from the moment they stepped across the threshold, they were treated like Hollywood royalty. The attention to detail was second to none—from the place settings through to the specially printed Valentine menus.

Rebecca ordered a grilled sole with all the trimmings and Alex took the veal. Before they had settled in and sipped their first cocktail, a violinist had serenaded her with what he assumed was an Italian folk tune. You knew this was a classy joint because the guy didn't ask for any money.

"We've been good together, haven't we?"

"Sure have, Rebecca. It's almost two years since we met."

"Again. Our boat ride to Coney Island when we were kids still leaves me with a smile when I think back to those times."

"I'm glad because for me that day was the beginning of the end, Rebecca—until you cruised into town on an overnight trip to stardom."

"Let me apologize for the way I treated you all those years ago, Alex. I did not understand about the world back then."

"None of us did—and no need to say you're sorry. I threatened your boyfriend to keep him away from you."

"My fiancé, you mean."

"Yeah. That wasn't right of me either."

"I always knew it was you, but nobody had any proof. I resented you for a long time after that."

"Rebecca, who wouldn't? That's water under the bridge. The amazing thing is that we are with each other now."

He gazed into her eyes–a warm glow in his belly from being in the same room as her. Then he pondered the impossible question of whether he felt more deeply for Rebecca or Sarah—and shook himself out of his reverie. He was divorced from Sarah, and Rebecca was his present for the evening. She had literally given herself to him earlier.

"We are fools under the stars and they watch us and laugh."

"Who said that?"

"It's from a show I was in when the Yiddish theater was still a thing on Broadway."

"Did you play a duchess or a princess?"

"Neither; second maid, but they were beautiful lines even though I didn't speak them."

Alex smiled and they held hands while the waiter cleared their plates and offered them cheesecake on the house. When that course was polished off, the couple continued to talk and stare out of the window. Despite Alex's late booking, they had the best table in the place.

"It's quiet around here. There's hardly been a car go by."

"Almost as though we weren't in a city like Vegas, Rebecca."

She sneaked a glance at him and carried on staring outside into the night.

"There are still too many lights to see the stars properly."

"We could nip out to the desert if you like. Five minutes further north and we'll be in the middle of nowhere."

"Would you mind, Alex?"

"Who's complaining? A guy with his girl, alone in the dark. Sounds good to me."

ALEX GRABBED A blanket from the trunk and covered Rebecca's shoulders as they stepped away from his car and stood in awe of the pitch black which engulfed them. With an arm over her shoulder, he stared upward and within a few seconds, small pinpricks of light emerged from the night's sky and they played a game of spotting different shapes in the twinkling stars.

"Rebecca, I don't believe they are laughing at us. Not tonight. Maybe they are smirking at the johns in Vegas, but they are grinning at you and me."

"Do you think so?"

"I am looking at them right now, aren't I? I've seen enough of this world to know how it feels to be laughed at—and I'm not feeling that. Are you?"

"I suppose not, Alex."

Their conversation trailed off as the two stared at the patterns up above. Every so often, Rebecca would point at a string of lights and explain to him the name of the constellation they were from and give him the ancient Greek story that went along with it. He'd had no idea she was filled with such knowledge.

"How long have you been fascinated by astrology?"

"By astronomy—since I was a little girl. When we were on the boat coming over to America, there was one night when I got to look out of the window in the middle of the Atlantic Ocean. And in the midst of the horror of that crossing was a single moment of light— when I saw the stars and imagined being a million miles away from that ship and the verstinkener families crammed into that tiny space."

He kissed her on the forehead and they embraced for a short while before Rebecca's gaze headed upward again. Another fifteen minutes and they both felt the cold of the night seep into the bodies and Alex suggested they return to the city. With chattering teeth, she agreed, and by the time they drove back to the parking lot at the Frontier, feeling had returned to all their fingers.

"Do you fancy a nightcap in the bar or shall we go straight back to the cottage, Rebecca?"

"A cocktail to warm our souls might be lovely."

He drove into his named space twenty feet from the hotel entrance and leaned over to kiss Rebecca as a car backfired in the distance. Alex tensed for a second, instincts on overdrive, and then relaxed. They sauntered over to the entrance with its revolving doors and two uniformed doormen, eager to help and ready to receive a gratuity for their services.

Arm draped on her shoulder, Alex looked up at the sky once more and Rebecca stopped to do the same.

"You still sure the stars aren't laughing, Alex?"

The headlights of a parked car switched to full beam and white light engulfed the couple. An engine sparked to life and the vehicle lurched forward, turning sharply to avoid Alex and Rebecca.

Then brakes screeched the saloon to a halt next to them. Alex twisted round to find out what was going on as the passenger window wound down and a black metal barrel emerged. He hit the dirt because his life depended on it, and as the first shot rang out, Alex used the momentum of his descent to drag Rebecca along with him.

As soon as he landed, he seized his pistol from his jacket and squeezed out a slug at the passenger who retaliated with second and third bullets. Then the car squealed off, out of the parking lot and into the night.

Alex stood up, holding his piece in both hands, firing slugs at the all-too-distant vehicle. When the gun was spent, Alex turned round to find both doormen kneeling next to Rebecca. He blinked, shut his eyes and stared out again. Red seeped onto the concrete forming a pool around Rebecca's limp body. Alex closed his ears to the screaming around him and zeroed in on his love's death throes. He pushed the doormen aside and held her still-warm body. Blood gushed from Rebecca's head and pulsed out of her chest. A well of emptiness engulfed the pit of his stomach as the gnawing understanding flowed through his head. Alex had lost the woman he loved more than life itself.

22

ALEX BURIED REBECCA in the Woodlawn Cemetery on Las Vegas Boulevard two days later. Although it tore his insides apart, he was forced to wait more than twenty-four hours for the initial police findings before he got the paperwork together and the ceremony organized. Garnett tried to intercede on his behalf, but the sheriff held little sway with the city force—and they saw no reason to speed up their process for a gangster Jew.

On Wednesday she was laid to rest, and that afternoon Alex received telegrams of condolence from Meyer and Charlie Lucky, who was still stuck in Sing Sing with no hope of parole. By Thursday, Alex was in a blue funk which stayed with him for the remainder of the week and only lifted when he thought about the shootist. He called Ezra and Massimo to his cottage—he hadn't left his home since he returned from the burial. Benny and Mickey had attended, along with Massimo and Ezra.

A handful of the hoofers had also turned up at the funeral out of respect for Rebecca and in acknowledgment of Alex's importance in the casino community. He had paid for a rabbi to come over from Los Angeles to officiate the ceremony, and Benny had ensured ten Jewish men were present to make the shiva—the evening prayers—kosher. That night, Alex cried his eyes out like a little boy and only spoke with the reception desk to order room service over the next two days.

"What have you found out for me?"

"The saloon had out-of-town plates. One of Garnett's men pulled a similar vehicle over about twenty minutes after the hit for speeding and let them go on their way. Nothing wrong there because the medical examiner hadn't even pronounced her dead at that point."

Ezra glanced at Massimo and wondered if he'd overstepped the mark at all, but his friend nodded and Ezra continued.

"There were two men and Waterman gave me good descriptions of both of them."

"Denzel Waterman?"

"You know him?"

"Our paths have crossed, but no mind. Anyone recognize them?"

"I called back east and Meyer is checking whether there is a Brownsville connection."

Alex nodded at the implication that this might have been a hit with instructions issued out of the Bronx—his old home from home.

"Is there much of Murder Corporation left?"

"Not like it was when you were in charge, Alex. But there is still a need to settle disputes between syndicate members, and there's a pool of fellas willing to pull a trigger for a price."

"I assume the hit was aimed at me. Rebecca never mentioned anybody who might do her harm."

"Correct, Alex. You were the target and for reasons we can't explain, the guy missed you and caught her instead."

"Twice. One in the chest, another in the head."

"In which direction was the car heading when Waterman let it go?"

"Los Angeles, but we all know that doesn't guarantee it was their destination. They could have turned around and hightailed it through town ten minutes later. No one was on the lookout for a black saloon with unknown assailants then—apart from you and the doormen."

Alex swirled his Scotch in its glass and knocked back the remains of the contents.

"As soon as you find the location of either of the two men, you tell me. Day or night—I don't care. You hear me?"

"Loud and clear, boss."

THE SCENE PLAYING out before Alex was the same as so many situations where he, Ezra, and Massimo had discussed matters with an assailant in an empty warehouse in the middle of the Lower East Side. The only difference was that the location was in the heart of the desert, where nobody passed by to hear the screams of any prisoner. And that was how Alex wanted it.

Trussed on the floor was a guy in a black suit and white shirt, his mouth stuffed with Massimo's handkerchief bound with twine. The sound of the man's nostrils inhaling and exhaling filled the open space—a single-story shack reached via a solitary track running from the highway.

Alex had got a call from Ezra to tell him that one of his fellas in Los Angeles had dropped a dime and suggested they pay a visit to Rico Piovene, who had come into money and boasted of its origins. Ezra and Massimo had driven to the City of Angels, grabbed the guy, thrown him into their trunk, and brought him to his current location.

"Sit him upright so we can converse like men."

Alex dragged a wooden chair next to Piovene's body and let his lieutenants haul the man up and dump him on the seat—making sure his wrists remained tied behind his back. While they sorted out the wheezing captive, Alex found more furniture so everybody could be seated if they wanted, although the other two remained standing to tower over Piovene.

"Do you know who I am?"

A shake of the head.

"Do you know where you are?"

A second no.

"Any idea why you are here?"

Naught for three.

"For a guy who's opened his mouth in a Los Angeles bar telling the world about your business, you don't know much, do you?"

Alex stared into Rico's eyes, spearing into his soul—not letting his gaze break, even for a second.

"My friend tells me you came into some gelt. Did good fortune smile on you?" Alex indicated to Massimo that Piovene needed to speak and to remove his handkerchief. "I asked you a question and unless you want a beating, you'd better give me an answer."

Rico looked at the two lieutenants and returned to staring at Alex.

"Yeah, I got some money. What business is it of yours?"

"We will get to that in a minute."

"I didn't catch your name, Mac."

Before Alex responded, Ezra stepped toward him. "That's Alex Cohen, you schnook." And he landed a punch in the stomach before Rico could digest the information.

They waited for Piovene to recover from the blow for a minute.

"Now you know who I am, you should be aware of what forces I can unleash against you. So let us try again. Why do you think you are here?"

"I must have displeased you."

"Interesting understatement. Any idea what that might have been?"

Piovene shrugged and stared into the middle distance, just above Alex's shoulder.

"I ain't done nothing."

"If that is so, why were you telling anybody in earshot that you'd earned money from a Vegas hit a few days ago?"

"I say things, but it don't have to be true."

"So you weren't involved in a hit?"

"Not me. You got me confused with some other fella."

"Rico, I want you to understand something, so listen carefully. Everyone in this room knows what you have done. That is not the issue. What I have to decide is what'll happen to you because of your involvement in the hit. And that depends on what you say and what you do during this conversation."

"I have already said it was not me."

"Let's pretend for a minute you are telling me the truth. We know you're not, but work with me here. If it wasn't from the hit, where did your extra gelt come from?"

"I won it on the horses."

"Gambling? And yet you told the bar you'd been to Vegas on a hit, like you were a big shot."

"I ran my mouth off and I'd been drinking. The story sounded better than I picked a horse and it came in first."

"Did you pull the trigger or was it the other guy?"

"It wasn't me. I placed a bet and it came good."

"If you were the driver, then I will let you live. If you continue to lie to me, then I cannot guarantee the state of your health."

Alex remained silent for a minute to give Piovene a chance to think through his situation and to make the right decision.

"Well? I have given you an opportunity to reconsider your ridiculous story. Were you the trigger man?"

"The driver."

"That's better. There's nothing worse than having your intelligence insulted. Who carried out the hit?"

"Art Nicchi."

Alex turned to Massimo. "You heard of this guy?"

"No, but it won't be hard to find him."

"Well done, Rico. Now here is one more question and then you can go."

A smile flitted across Piovene's face.

"Who hired you?"

"Art asked me to help him with some out-of-town business. He didn't say who was paying the bill and I didn't ask. You know how it is."

"That I do, Rico. Are you sure this Nicchi didn't mention a name at all?"

"If I could tell you, I would, because I want to get out of this place alive."

"You're a stand-up man, Rico, and I believe you. Art was the brains of the outfit and couldn't trust you with the name of the person who hired you."

"Am I free to go then?"

Alex smiled and stood up.

"There's just one more thing, Rico."

He walked over and bent over the man as if to have a private word, whispering to him so that neither Ezra nor Massimo heard.

"For you, this was business and if Art'd only clipped me, then that would be the end of the matter. But you guys made the mistake of killing my childhood sweetheart."

Alex straightened up, pulled his piece from its resting place in his jacket, jammed the barrel in Rico Piovene's mouth, and shot him in the head. Blood splattered out the rear of his skull and the body lurched backward, falling on the floor.

"Bring me Art Nicchi and make sure no harm befalls the momzer before I speak with him."

23

THREE DAYS LATER and Piovene's body was no longer lying in a bloody mess on the floor. Most of him was in a shallow grave a mile away from the shack. Now in Rico's seat was Art Nicchi—a man sufficiently smart not to inform Rico who was paying the bills but not clever enough to leave the country and never return.

"Art, you know why you are here so let's get to it. Who hired you to kill me?"

"Cohen, you should understand I can't tell you."

"There is a world of difference between not being able to do something and refusing to do it. You assassinated someone very dear to me, and there are consequences."

"The skirt?"

"My girlfriend. My childhood sweetheart. Yes."

Ezra glanced at Massimo—they hadn't known Alex and Rebecca's lives stretched back to their days in the Bowery.

"And, Art. I need to understand why she died. Rico told me you were the hired hand and he was the driver. Is that correct?"

"I pulled the trigger, but I can't say who paid me."

"I suppose they never gave you a name. Just a middleman acting on behalf of a silent partner."

"Lying to you won't do me any good. I owed a Shylock some money—way more than chump change—and they passed my betting slip up the chain until it landed on a certain someone's desk. He told me I could wipe the slate clean if I did one job for him."

"How d'you obtain the gelt to pay Rico?"

"What I was being asked was priced higher than my sizeable debt so there was spare on the top. I gave most of that to Rico because I figured he'd helped me get out of a big hole."

"And now he's dropped you into an even bigger one."

"Sure looks like it."

"You walk out of here by giving me a name. Anything less and we get to work on you. Understand?"

"Listen, Mac. If I give up my boss today, you will find me in a ditch next week."

Alex smiled. "And if I don't hear the name this afternoon, you'll be buried in the desert by nightfall. Your options are limited and unpleasant—unless you spill who needed me dead."

Nicchi stared out and kept his lips shut. Alex could tell he wished to say, but old allegiances die hard and the guy hadn't dealt with the fact that Alex needed more than the organ grinder—he wanted revenge on this monkey too.

"Art, I'm giving you one last chance to offer me the name before I insist on you saying. Who put out the hit and was it authorized by the syndicate?"

"Oh no. This was a local matter from what I understand, but I won't give up who."

Alex believed Nicchi and knew that within the next sixty minutes, the guy would sell the souls of his grandchildren as yet unborn to stop the pain Alex was about to inflict. He stood up and walked over to two bags lying on the floor twenty feet away. One was a sack and the other a tool bag. He yanked Piovene's head from the sack, dumping it on Nicchi's lap, causing the man to scream with fear. Then Alex removed a hammer from the tool kit and slammed it into Nicchi's right knee.

AN HOUR LATER and Art Nicchi fell back into unconsciousness and Alex had what he was looking for; Jack Dragna had called for the hit.

The guy who owned Los Angeles wanted him dead even though they'd met only once, and then Benny had done almost all the talking. It made little sense.

"Throw some water on him," Alex instructed and Nicchi was dowsed with a bucket and came round. Alex grabbed him by the hair as he sat, strapped to the chair, fingers and toes broken, torso slashed several times, and cigarette burns on his hands and feet.

"I woke you up to let you know that you will die."

Alex executed Art Nicchi with a single shot to the head and then he stepped back three paces. Ezra and Massimo moved in, cut off the straps that bound the man to his seated position and the corpse fell to the floor and splashed into the bloody pool which had formed over the intervening hours since his arrival.

"Is it too much to send their heads to Dragna?"

"Yes, Alex. Please don't let your anger overcome you."

"I know. It's more important to get to the bottom of why the hit was called than have revenge for Rebecca."

"The body count is rising, Alex. I doubt if she'd want you to kill more people in her name. You've buried her, and Massimo and I will make this carcass vanish for you. Go home and let us do our jobs."

Ezra was right. Rebecca was dead and nothing he did would bring her back to life and he must deal with Dragna. Alex needed to figure out how he had offended the boss of LA.

"BENNY, WHY WOULD Jack Dragna want me dead?"

Siegel sipped his coffee and settled back in the seat positioned behind his desk in his office. Alex sat opposite, barely able to concentrate on the matter at hand, his loss sitting in the pit of his stomach like a bowl of lokshen.

"Alex, it isn't anything personal—he hardly knows you. So it must be business."

He thought for a minute and tried to list their interests in common. His mind was blank on the matter as snippets of conversation with Rebecca wafted into his head instead.

"There's prostitution, the hotel, a casino, and the racing wire. Anything else you run, Alex?"

"That's about all." His voice trailed off, dulled by sadness. "But it's only the news wire that goes beyond the city boundary. The rest is local."

"Let me have a talk with him and see what's going on. If it is the wire, then I wonder why he didn't attack me too."

"Benny, you are a member of the syndicate and I am not. I was a much easier mark."

"And you won't be able to get your revenge either for the same reason, Alex."

"I am painfully aware of that, but we buried the trigger man and the driver in the desert."

"May Rebecca rest in peace."

Alex drilled a hole in Benny's head with his eyes—did Siegel mean what he had said? He had been the one to try it on with her, and Alex had never called him on that. He had respected Rebecca's wishes to not pursue the matter, but it had not sat right with him. And here was another occasion involving her when he wouldn't be able to act the way he wanted.

MARCH 1944

24

"WE'RE FIGHTING THE Japs and Nazis now. Sometimes I wonder if I should have enlisted again and returned to France."

Alex and Benny sat by the pool in El Rancho as the late afternoon sun headed toward the horizon.

"I thought you had enough of the army life in the Great War. You told me that experience broke you."

"True, but I went over there hoping to save Jewish lives. I might have been wrong last time, but Hitler means our people only harm. We need to stand up to him."

Benny sipped at his cocktail and considered Alex's suggestion, then shook his head.

"War is a young man's game. I met Goebbels before the war started, when I was involved in a spot of gun-running—total prick for sure. But the reports you hear are that the Nazis have internment camps for the Jews. You fighting on a beach ain't going to save anyone from those workhouses."

"Don't you want to do something though?"

"You earned yourself a Purple Heart last time. Leave it for some other upstart to take the glory."

"There are people closer to home who are dying too."

Benny eyed Alex, checked his watch, and intoned, "Louis must be dead by now."

Alex raised his glass to make a simple toast. "To Louis Buchalter, syndicate member, Murder Corporation director, and friend to Benny Siegel. Rest in peace."

"Please God, may we be in Israel next year."

Even though Alex had thrown Abe Reles out of the Half Moon window, there was other testimony and other murders that had brought Louis to his knees. Now he would be remembered as the first gangster to fry in the mercy seat.

"Do you feel responsible, Alex?"

"What do you mean?"

"The Rosen hit—that's what Reles testified about and that was one of yours, I thought."

"Yes and no. I carried out the contract, but Louis issued the instructions to me in front of Reles. I barely remember, but the fella walked in and out of our meetings in Brownsville. Stupid thing is that if Anastasia hadn't been so keen to choose the venue, we'd have been in Lindy's and Reles would have heard jack."

"I know you were inside, but Louis gave himself up to the Feds in thirty-nine. He'd been on the lam for a year or two."

"Then he was a fool. If I'd been him, I would have left the country —or the state at the very least. Sometimes a field in Wisconsin can be appealing."

Benny smiled because Alex was right, even though he was talking ill of a guy he'd known since he was a kid.

"The afternoon edition said that they flipped the switch on Alfonse's brother after they did for Louis."

"Well, Alex, at least Alfonse won't bear the pain of hearing about the death."

"Brains like mush."

The men soaked in the decaying rays of the setting sun as they considered the deaths surrounding the people in their lives. After several minutes, Alex broke the silence.

"Did you get anywhere with Jack Dragna?"

"You've met him…"

"Briefly…"

"And you must pick your moments with him. He is liable to fly off and act crazy."

"We are talking about the man who organized a hit on me and ended up killing my girlfriend."

"I know, but as soon as the time is appropriate, I'll speak with him. From what you found out, this was business and that makes it to do with the wire service. For Jack to strike out like that means we are doing something right and he feels threatened."

"Lashing out at me was not the way to go, Benny."

"No, of course not—but we have to carry on, even if we apply a level of caution. His actions might have set us back a small amount, but there is an enormous amount of money to make from Trans-American."

Alex had expected more from Benny than a half-promise to speak to Dragna at some point. This was a syndicate matter as the guy was attacking one of Meyer's key investments. There must be some reason he didn't want to push things harder, and Alex doubted it was because Siegel was worried whether his erstwhile underling would get his nose put out of joint.

That night, Alex lit a remembrance candle for Alfonse's brother but refused to do anything to commemorate Buchalter's demise. Just because the fella was dead didn't mean how he'd behaved when he was alive was any different.

JUNE 1945

25

ALEX STAYED AWAY from the war in the Pacific and the one raging against the Jews in Europe. For reasons best known to himself, Benny stayed away from Jack Dragna and Rebecca's death faded from everyone's minds apart from Alex's.

Six weeks after peace was declared across Europe, Moe Sedway and Gus Greenbaum arrived in Vegas to manage Benny's latest acquisition: the El Cortez resort on East Fremont. This venue had all you'd expect from a Siegel establishment—casino, hotel rooms, and prostitutes, restaurants, a stage with dancing girls, and a lot more besides.

"I will turn this joint around and make it as successful as the dumps I've seen in Texas."

"What's the difference between this place and El Rancho?"

Alex admired Benny's reach but was concerned that the fella's attention should be focused on the racing wire, which had languished over the past year, rather than expanding his entertainment interests. That said, Benny had wanted to create a gaming empire here twenty years ago, so Alex shouldn't have been surprised by the way Siegel's head was turning.

"I'll refurbish the interior so there's a lot less Mexican ranch to the place. We want to appeal to the johns who live on the coasts of this great nation, not just those who have a land border in the south."

"Benny, you sure are living the dream."

"It's the American way, right? I'm making a million a year out of El Rancho and Trans-American. By next year I want to double that—and again, every year until nobody can touch me."

ALEX DIDN'T QUESTION where Benny got the money to make the purchase–he received a cool half a million from the news wire annually—and as an equal partner, Benny was getting the same. The rest of Benny's income was a mystery, not that it was any of Alex's business what Benny earned.

Gus and Moe came across as upright fellas when Alex met them a few days later. They had a classic New York Jewish mobster feel to them—gray flannel suits and fedora hats. Their eyes burned with suspicion but, to hear them talk, you'd think they were ordinary businessmen with a hawklike eye on profit margins. For those who cared to look, the bulges in their jacket pockets showed they packed heat.

"Benny wants to run an elite joint for the high spenders in the country. But Moe and I think we can all make more money by opening the place up to anybody with some greenbacks. He's the boss, so we'll do whatever he says."

Moe nodded in agreement and Alex smiled. The three were having a coffee in El Rancho, comped by Benny as always.

"Benny has a nose for gaming, that's for sure. When I first met him in New York, he talked about building a casino out west with a deck of cards and a piece of green baize."

"Alex, that's funny because he carried that story around with him wherever he went. I must admit I thought the idea was goofy, but what did I know?"

"Moe, the fellas back east never took Benny seriously and now look at us all."

"MEYER. HOW'S THE hustle and bustle of New York?"
"All is good here, Alex."

"Pleased to hear it. And how is your accounts clerk doing?"

"Sarah is well—I've promoted her to my executive secretary. I shall let her know you inquired after her health."

"No need to bother her, Meyer. Was this a social call or have we something to discuss?"

"How is business, Alex?"

"Are you on your own or have you put me on a squawk box?"

"Both. I wanted to drink my coffee and speak at the same time."

"Meyer, the Last Frontier is doing well—and Trans-American is catching up. As you know, it has taken much longer than anyone thought to make it work outside of Vegas, but we are getting there. I'm going on a sales trip soon to break open San Francisco—there has been interference from Jack Dragna which has slowed us down, but Benny must have kept you apprised of all that."

"I'm sure he has. Can you be more precise for me? I want figures, Alex."

"You know my numbers because I always show my appreciation, right? There's half a million from Trans-American and the Frontier generates about the same for me, including my interests in prostitution."

"How about El Rancho?"

"I can't be certain but I would expect El Rancho to clear more than the Last Frontier—it's bigger and better established."

"That's what I thought—very helpful. And as far as you are aware, El Rancho is profitable?"

"Yes. Is there something I should know, Meyer?"

"How are Moe and Gus? Have they settled in yet?"

"We've helped them secure places to stay and they seem fine—but they've only been here a handful of days, so it's too early to say."

"They'll find their feet soon enough. Good guys."

Alex put the phone down. Meyer knew all the numbers at every second of the day or night—he had no need to hear it from Alex. Instead, he wanted to listen to him speak the sums out loud. And the way he changed the topic when Alex asked if anything was up showed him that there was something going on—only Meyer didn't want to talk about it.

◆ ◆ ◆

ALEX CALCULATED BENNY'S income and the difference between what he'd told Alex a few days before and the implications from Meyer that El Rancho wasn't wiping its own ass. If Alex was right, Benny was underplaying how much he was making to the syndicate, because Meyer implied there was little money coming out of the resort.

These thoughts lingered in his mind the next time he hooked up with Mickey. Almost like the rear booth at Lindy's, Alex took his seat at a table by the El Rancho pool, only there was no need to have any of their lieutenants sit by the entrance because the local cops were in their pocket and there were no rival gangs in town.

"How's tricks, Mickey?"

"All going fine, Alex."

"My prostitution numbers have flatlined these past two months. Has the casino income suffered the same way?"

"Nah. Since the start of the year, things have picked up. We might be in the middle of a war, but the high rollers are still piling into town and gambling like there's no tomorrow."

"Is that only in the hotel or are takings up with the other bookies?"

"Across the board. Why d'you ask?"

"No reason. I was just wondering where we should expand our efforts with Trans-American. We can gouge more in Vegas or hop on a train someplace else."

"Buy your ticket today. This town is full—I'd be surprised if there is a single track bookmaker in the city limits who isn't paying us through the nose. Where are you thinking of going?"

"The two hottest options are San Francisco or Los Angeles."

"You and Dragna have unfinished business, right?"

"That's one way of putting it, Mickey. Could I count on your support if I were to go after Dragna?"

"I beat him to the punch when I came over here to work with Benny, but Jack and I go back years and as much as I disagree with what he did to you and your skirt…"

"Rebecca."

"Whatever… that still doesn't mean I want to raise a gun to the fella's face."

"And what about Benny?"

Mickey laughed. "Well, I ain't going to be firing no shot at him either."

"No, I meant, how would you feel if you'd heard that Benny was making a little on the side from your hard work?"

"I wouldn't be happy—who would? But is that what you are saying is happening because whoever's pouring out those kinds of rumors needs seeing to. Does Benny know these lies are flying about town?"

"One barfly spouting his mouth off is not worth lifting a finger over, Mickey. I was just thinking out loud and nothing more."

"Well, do it in your head and don't let your lips move so much."

Alex marveled at Mickey's loyalty to Benny—and how poor he was at counting. The amount of money Benny said he was making far exceeded anything that Mickey was seeing, but it did not rankle with him. Perhaps he didn't care what his boss did, provided he himself was in gravy, but Alex minded and Meyer had chosen him as the person to talk to on the matter.

26

EZRA, MASSIMO, AND Alex took a train to San Francisco and grabbed a hire car at the other end—there's nothing like local plates to stop heads from turning when you drive down the street. They spent the first week creating a map of the bookies—just as they had when they tried to open up Los Angeles. In stark contrast to the earlier attempt to break new ground, Alex also chose to piece together who ran the different parts of the city before making a move.

Anthony Lima had been running the town for about ten years, although he had focused his attention on extortion and prostitution. Alex arranged an appointment with Lima and brought with him a bottle of imported Italian wine.

"Thank you for taking the time to see me, Mr. Lima."

"I am happy to be with a friend of Benny's and, please, call me Anthony."

"Your time is precious and I do not wish to waste a drop of it. There is a business proposition I'd like to offer you."

"Let's crack open your vino and I will hear what you have to say."

"The syndicate is making a significant investment in the Trans-American racing wire and we want to introduce it in San Francisco. My understanding is that you do not have long tentacles in gaming, otherwise I would not be so presumptuous as to come here at all."

"Alex, what little betting takes place in my city isn't worth my while. If one day it becomes significant, I shall dip my beak in that trough."

"Anthony, I have mapped out where all the track bookies do business in town and I want to make them Trans-American customers. This will benefit me, naturally, but also the syndicate, and I would like to ensure our interests are aligned by sharing revenues with you personally."

Anthony smiled because he'd heard what happened when Alex tried to muscle into Jack Dragna's territory with the racing wire—it took him years to recover from that slapping.

"You have considered this well and I am always interested in making money, so what would be my end?"

"Like everyone else, I give my tithe to the syndicate to show appreciation. I am offering you ten percent of my gross share and I am asking you to do nothing in return—apart from allow me free passage around town as I generate gelt for the pair of us."

"You are a thoughtful and caring man—I wish there were more like you in this world, but a tithe is not much to offer. I understand it is proposed with respect, but I have lived without gambling revenues fine so far. Twenty percent would elicit a different response from me."

Alex smiled because Anthony was negotiating over price and that meant he was hooked.

"Fifteen percent is my highest offer—no matter what amount we agree, I still have fixed expenses that must be met. A racing wire is an expensive operation and there are other cities I could go to."

Anthony raised a hand to signal he had heard enough of Alex's spiel.

"I can live with that. You are offering me free money, after all."

"You better believe it."

WITH LIMA ON his side, Alex had received the green light to exploit gambling in San Francisco as much as he was able, but he knew two things—his priority was Trans-American and as soon as any other gaming revenues became significant then Anthony would step in and take it for his own.

The map of bookies in his hand, Alex instructed his lieutenants to hover around and see which were taking any serious racetrack bets. The other aspect for consideration was how susceptible the guys would be to buying from Trans-American. A second week and the three men assembled in Alex's hotel room—they'd had the good sense to bring in coffees and cake for the afternoon's meet.

"The important thing is to close the deal with every bookmaker in the city—I don't care who does it or how it is done. The contract is what we require."

"So we can use as much encouragement as we need?"

"No corpses, Massimo—and they must pay each week without us having to chase them for the gelt. It's the same as any other racket we've ever been in. We need them to bend to our will and not break."

All three men knew what was expected and how far to press a man before he'd reach for a gun or throw a punch. With Lima's backing, Alex hoped they'd meet less resistance than in LA.

"YOU THINK A bunch of Jews from Vegas will scare me more than a bunch of Italians from Chicago? Get outta here."

Alex, Ezra, and Massimo stood in front of their last catch of the morning, a guy who ran a book at the back of a bar overlooking the bay. Tourists and locals alike popped in and placed a wager with Luke, who didn't bat an eyelid when the three men approached him with their proposition.

"We are offering you the chance to get in on the ground up with a new wire service."

"I got one already and I make a pretty penny out of it. I don't need two."

"We aren't suggesting you use both—you should replace your current provider with Trans-American."

Alex had seen this conversation play out three times before on the same day and could sense how it would end up.

"I'll buy from you if you are much cheaper and the Chicago outfit tells me they are happy for me to do so—otherwise you're putting me in an impossible situation."

"We are backed by Anthony Lima and he would like you to go with Trans-American."

"I'm sure he would, but he doesn't have to deal with no Chicago mobsters, does he?"

Alex sighed—it had been the same all day. The most lucrative bookies were signed up to Ragen's Nationwide wire and coercing them to join Trans-American wouldn't mean they'd stay for very long. In fact, the only way would be to install a team of heavies in San Francisco to shake down each payment out of every bookmaker in town. This was not a viable business proposition from Alex's perspective.

They left Luke to give him time to reconsider his position and with a veiled threat they'd burn his home down and attack his family, but from what he'd said the Chicago outfit had made similar claims and not acted on them either.

"We might as well split up—three of us standing in front of one gonif just wastes time."

ALEX'S NEXT PORT of call was Frederico, who perched in the back of a bar near the Golden Gate Bridge, not that this meant he was any more amenable to the Trans-American service.

"Don't get me wrong, mister. If you were the only game in town, I'd buy from you—but the Nationwide got to me first. I've seen what they are capable of and have no interest in encouraging them to come to visit me."

"And a beating from them at some point is worse than a definite bashing from me later on today?"

"No disrespect, but I'd suggest not—just because the Nationwide fellas won't stop demanding money from me, no matter what I say."

"Frederico, how about this? Let me install our service for free. You use it without charge for three months, and then we can talk about our fees again."

"Put it in but I won't switch it on. The Nationwide will crack my skull open and I'll be lucky to wake up in a hospital."

That evening, the Vegas men shared war stories over a bite to eat.

"The Chicago mob has tied up this city tight—no wonder Lima was so susceptible to you coming into town, boss."

"Ezra, Anthony sure was happy for us to do the donkey work— now it makes sense. He'd already ceded gambling over to Chicago before we arrived."

"What are we going to do, Alex?"

"Let's stick to our original plan and keep hustling for a week and then we can take stock. If we've made little headway, then a fresh approach will be needed. The syndicate appears to be split into two factions with competing interests around the two wire services and we sure don't want to get caught in the middle of that shitstorm."

27

WHEN ALEX CAME back to Vegas, Benny was in no mood to hear about the inability of Trans-American to take hold in San Francisco. Instead, his head was filled with desire for a new woman in his life—Virginia Hill. Benny had brought his family over from New York when he first relocated, but like many powerful men, this never stopped him from playing around. He kept a mistress even though she was based in Beverly Hills and Mrs. Siegel was ensconced in Arcadia out in the San Gabriel Valley, Los Angeles.

Alex had a vague memory of seeing Virginia tending to some men when he visited Alfonse, and she had a history with the Chicago outfit before she ran prostitution in Mexico for some other of the syndicate's interests. But Alex did not judge her on how she earned a living—he didn't operate at that level, especially as his ex-wife was a former nafka, his mistress back then was an opium fiend, and his most recent girlfriend had been in the chorus line. None of these jobs could be mistaken for anything respectable. Yet at some point, to a greater or lesser extent, he had loved them all—although not at the same point.

They met over a cocktail, much as Alex might have predicted, by the pool in El Rancho. Benny was beaming and besotted—Alex couldn't remember seeing the man so happy.

"So how did you guys meet?"

"Charlie introduced us in New York years before."

"And then we bumped into each other again at a Hollywood party two weeks ago."

Benny looked at Hill as she added the detail to provide the information Alex wanted to know—how long had they been dating and why had she flashed onto the scene in Las Vegas. Alex nodded approval and Benny ordered another round of drinks.

"Do you act, Virginia?"

"I got myself an agent, but I'm between roles right now."

"And who held the party where you met again?"

Benny and Virginia looked at each other, neither wanting to go first. In the end, Siegel relented. "George Raft threw one of his blowout affairs and we got together that evening, but we've known each other off and on for years."

Alex was teasing Benny because the couple had been seeing each other ever since Hill was sent by Charlie Lucky from Chicago to New York to keep tabs on syndicate member Joe Adonis back in 1937. Their relationship had been a closely guarded secret, although Charlie informed Alex and Meyer after Hill arrived in town so they'd know not to stoke any unnecessary fires with Benny.

"For a woman who wants to smash into the movies, you got a low profile in Hollywood, Virginia."

"I should change my agent."

"You just haven't had your big break yet, Virginia."

"Kind of you to say so, Benny, but I've been to enough auditions to know these producers are interested in me, but not for a part in their movie, if you get my drift."

Benny ground his molars at the thought of another man laying a hand on his skirt and Alex marveled at the double standard—given how Benny had behaved toward Rebecca—when he had his wife at home and Virginia in an LA apartment somewhere.

"I am sure your talent will reveal itself soon." Was Alex's acid remark aimed at Virginia, who slept with anybody the syndicate instructed her to or with Benny and the old scars still unhealed?

"Shall we go for a bite to eat? There's a new Mexican opened up nearby, which is meant to be awesome."

"Sure, Benny, but if you two want to be alone together, I'll understand."

"Of course you're welcome, Alex. Isn't he, babe?"

"Yep."

Virginia stared at Alex when she spoke, her eyes beaming into the back of his skull, almost like she was trying to convey some other meaning than what she said. Alex took her at face value, at least for now.

◆ ◆ ◆

THE RESTAURANT WAS fine but nothing special despite the hype. By the time dessert was served, in a perfunctory manner given the importance of the men sat at the table, several bottles of wine had been consumed and neither Benny nor Alex took offense. Virginia's indignation made up for both of them.

"You're not going to pay the gratuity, are you? I thought we'd need a catcher's mitt for our entrees."

"It's not the waiter's fault."

"Benny, who do you think is responsible for the delivery of the food from the kitchen to our table?"

Alex remained silent during this lovers' spat. Virginia made a good point, and she knew Benny well enough to understand that was not how she would get him to change his mind—almost as if she was saying it to her audience rather than to Benny.

"I know how restaurants work, babe—I own two. If you want to decide on the tip, then pay for the meal, otherwise, it doesn't concern you."

Virginia opened up her purse and rifled through to see how much money she had on her. When her shoulders slumped to signify how little gelt there was, her indignation got the better of her and she lashed out.

"I don't know what you are staring at, Alex. If you were a gentleman, you'd have said something by now and told Benny how foolish he is being."

"Virginia, I make it a rule not to express an opinion in differences between two people as close as you and Benny. Second, Benny is my business partner and I have known him for twenty years. You and I met today, so I will show him more loyalty than you."

"You are useless, aren't you?"

She spat each word out with genuine venom and eyeballed Alex for five, ten seconds. He ignored the outburst, took a sip from his drink, and lit a cigarette, careful not to blow smoke in her face, despite his childish desire to do so.

Until this point, Virginia had appeared all right to hang out with, but now she had revealed a darker side to her. The stories Alex had heard of how she manipulated the rich and powerful men in her sway made more sense. There were tales of the Chicago outfit sending her off to sleep with bosses from other cities to find out their plans and to shift their opinions. She had been so good at that, they sent her to Mexico to run some narcotics angles down there.

The time she met Benny in New York was around when she was sleeping with Adonis—under instruction from Chicago. A high-class nafka with business talent, and now she had her clutches into Siegel.

Benny pulled out a roll of notes and put some down by his plate. Then he counted out a smaller amount and, while staring straight at Virginia, threw the second bunch on top of the first pile of greenbacks. His point made, Virginia tutted, grabbed her coat, and stormed out.

"I'd better go after her."

"If you say so, Benny."

He ran out of the restaurant and Alex smiled as he witnessed the couple through the glass frontage having a stand-up row in front of a room full of diners. Neither Sarah nor Rebecca had behaved like that. Then he waited until the fight was over before walking out the joint and taking a stroll back to the Frontier.

OCTOBER 1945

28

LAS VEGAS ATTRACTED many kinds to its city borders. The more astute money men recognized what Benny had known since the twenties—a resort where you could gamble, enjoy a decent meal, and sleep on the premises is a potential goldmine. Billy Wilkerson had a vision of a new hotel, focused on gambling with lodging rooms, a stage, and a restaurant.

He had only one issue—gelt. He calculated that the cost of the land combined with the build meant he was short by some way and the banks were not prepared to take on the risk—gaming was still a no-no for most of the country. Meyer Lansky came to town and met with Wilkerson, Benny, and Alex.

"So, Billy, on the phone you said you had funding issues that you wanted us to talk about."

Wilkerson looked around the table and shivered as he saw he was surrounded by these gang bosses. It is one thing to ask a known crime financier for money—it is quite another to be sitting face-to-face with the Jewish mob in your own hometown.

"This is the deal, Meyer. I own a thirty-three-acre plot south of the city line where I can develop my entertainment vision how I see fit without the Vegas elders sticking their noses in my affairs. The cost of materials has skyrocketed because of the war, and to achieve any return on my investment, I need to get the complex built and open."

"What makes you think your place will be successful so far away from the action?"

"No offense to El Rancho, El Cortez, or the Last Frontier but these are aimed at a different customer to mine. I want to reach the rich and the famous—develop a casino and hotel venue where you can smell the money dripping down the walls."

"Billy, I invested in El Cortez with the same aim as you, only I inherited the Tex-Mex facade. Our ideas are aligned and I would be happy to work with you on this new venture."

"Thanks, Benny. I have the advantage that I am starting with fields of dirt and nothing more."

"How much gelt are you seeking for the investment?"

"Meyer, to get the buildings up and ready for customers, hire staff, and open the doors? Six hundred thousand."

Billy eyed the three men and settled his gaze on Meyer. Nobody was showing any outward signs—these were not fellas to play poker with if you wanted to keep your shirt.

"You know what'll happen if you can't meet your financial obligations?"

Wilkerson gulped, imagined the worst, and nodded.

"Yes, that is clear to me."

"Punitive interest charged per day. When I invest, I want everybody to walk in with their eyes wide open."

"Sure, Meyer. I wouldn't come to you and ask for your help if I wasn't aware of the consequences of doing so."

"And what would be the size of my stake?"

"I thought you were offering me a loan?"

"Billy, you said you wanted an investment and I told you that was acceptable. If you prefer me as a creditor then we can reach an arrangement along those lines but I'll need collateral and the only thing worth my time and energy would be the thirty-three-acre site and I wouldn't release that until every dime was paid back. Plus my interest rate is not what a bank'd charge you—I have my costs to underwrite. So an investment is cheaper and safer for you. Once the place is up-and-running, you'll need everything to be plain sailing with unions and suppliers. And the last thing you want is for the place to burn down. My investment secures insurance against all these potential difficulties."

Meyer smiled at Billy, whose furtive glances at Benny and Alex showed he hadn't engaged with what it meant to do business with a syndicate member.

"Yes, an investment sounds the best option."

Benny cleared his throat. "Meyer, if you don't mind, I would like to put some money in myself."

"Fine by me, but only once Billy here tells us how big the stake will be."

"Fifty percent?"

"Without our capital, you have a gigantic pile of earth, some blueprints, and nothing much else, right?"

Wilkerson nodded agreement.

"In that case, our gelt is worth more than half of nothing. Let's pretend we asked for the whole thing, you refused and we end up with two-thirds. Would that save us wasting our time haggling?"

Another hard swallow from Billy and he consented.

"In the hope we'd come to an arrangement, I got Mendy Greenberg to draw up the paperwork for us. All we have to do is fill in the blanks for the cash sum and stake. You can have the money before you go to sleep tonight."

They shook hands on the deal and signed the contracts which Meyer whipped out of his briefcase.

"Benny and Alex will work with you to ensure everything runs like clockwork from now on—any problems then see them. They will be my eyes and ears on the ground."

Once Billy had thanked Meyer profusely, he walked off to leave the three men alone by the El Rancho pool. Meyer was the first to speak.

"Congratulations, Benny, we each own a third of the new hotel. What shall we call it?"

"That's easy, the Flamingo. It'll remind me of Virginia's lovely long legs every day I go to work."

Alex smiled because that was Hill's nickname, but most people called her that because her cheeks went flamingo pink when she hit the booze too hard.

"Works for me, Benny. The next item on the agenda is that you must buy out Wilkerson's remaining stake. We don't need this schnook to build and run a gambling joint. Reach an agreement with him by the end of the week or a terrible accident will befall him."

AFTER BENNY WENT back to his office to sort out some problem with a hotel guest, Alex asked Meyer if he could dip his beak in the Flamingo trough, but he would hear none of it.

"As much as I respect your desire to make money out of this matter, I must decline your request, Alex. The syndicate needs no other business partners."

"Is that what it comes down to, Meyer? I'm still not a member of the syndicate so you will shut me out of the juiciest deals."

"Be patient. There are reasons why you can be no part of this and they will become clear later, but until then you must bide your time and trust me, I have your best interests at heart."

"You don't make it easy for me."

"Alex, nobody told us life was a walk in the park."

MOE AND GUS were brought in so Benny could delegate the day-to-day activities and focus his attention on all the hotels under his ownership. Alex was asked to keep an eye on what the two men were doing, but they followed Benny's orders and Benny made all the decisions.

One of the first things he did was to stop buying from out of state. The architect's drawings were explicit and called for the finest of all materials, but Benny changed suppliers at almost every turn.

"Are you trying to make the investment capital stretch further, Benny?"

"What are you talking about, Alex?"

"The specification was for imported marble in the lobby, but it's only traveling from California. So I figure you're being careful with the syndicate's gelt."

"And what business is it of yours?"

"No disrespect—I was just asking."

"All you need to do is make sure Moe and Gus get on with their jobs—and nothing more."

"I haven't seen Virginia for a few days. Is everything all right between you two?"

"Alex, you're in a curious frame of mind tonight. She's off on some business for me in Paris if that's acceptable to you."

Alex gave up talking to Benny at that point. The next day he popped over to the airport and made a few inquiries. Virginia had flown out by private jet two days before, although the destination on the manifest was Geneva.

29

HILL'S RETURN TO Vegas was called through to Alex, who had asked a contact at the airport to keep a lookout for Benny's friend. When she arrived at El Rancho, Alex was already in the lobby and feigned surprise at bumping into her.

"How are you, Virginia?"

"Fine, thanks. What are you doing here, Alex?"

"Passing through. You know what it's like—there's always something to do for Benny."

"He likes to keep everybody busy, that's for sure."

"You've been out of town—I haven't seen you here for a while."

"Yeah…"

Her voice trailed off in abject disinterest.

"Do you have time for a quick drink, Virginia?"

"Well, I don't know…"

He smiled and looked in the general direction of the pool and the position of his usual table. Virginia hesitated and then shrugged in acceptance. Alex led her to the poolside and she slipped her sunglasses on. As they sat down, she ordered a cosmo and he asked for a coffee.

"Did you pop back to LA for a few days?"

"No, Alex. I was out of the country."

"Anywhere exotic?"

"I wouldn't say so—it depends if you are used to international travel."

"I've seen more than my fair share of France and Belgium."

"Really? I had you down as someone without a passport."

"Well, I don't have one of those."

"So how come?"

"I was stationed there during the war."

"No offense, but you were too old, weren't you? Besides, I'd have heard if you'd only recently got back from Europe."

It was Alex's turn to be confused until he realized Virginia's mistake.

"I was talking about the First World War, not the one just passed."

"That must have been quite something."

"Haunts me even now. They gave me a medal, but that is no substitute for returning home with all your friends in one piece."

"Did you leave many behind?"

"Far too many. Have you been to France?"

"Several times—I'd love to make Paris my second home."

"Yeah? Is that where you went on this trip?"

"No, I was elsewhere. Alex, why are you so interested in my travels?"

"To be honest, I am trying to look after Benny's interests and I don't want you to take this the wrong way, but I know that when you came back from wherever you went, your baggage was several pounds lighter. And that got me to thinking that perhaps you had left something behind."

"Did it? You're sounding like you are a cigarette paper away from accusing me."

"Not at all, Virginia—just commenting. If Benny is getting you to carry out errands, that is none of my business and I am not prying into his or your affairs."

"Funny, because that is what it sounds like you are doing."

"Nope—you must be mixing me up with some other fella. I'm only happy when Benny is happy and if you are facing any difficulties with these trips of yours, then all you need to do is ask and I'll be there for you."

She looked at him, trying to decide whether to believe him. Alex smiled back and sipped his coffee, which was cooling down.

"There is nothing to worry about, Alex. A few years ago I worked down south with some friends from Chicago and they have some interests in Switzerland, so I fly out to help them because, like you, they don't have a passport."

"Do they speak French over there?"

"Yes, they do, Alex."

He reckoned that meant she would be in Geneva rather than Zurich, where they spoke German. Alex's tour in Europe wasn't entirely spent in the trenches, despite the worst of his memories. And Geneva was renowned for its discreet private banks. Either Virginia was squirreling cash away for the Chicago outfit or the source of the gelt was closer to home. Besides, Alex would have known if there were regular Italian Illinois visitors in town.

ALEX LAY IN bed that night–not everything Virginia had told him added up. The Chicago outfit supported James Ragen's news wire, and Benny was in direct competition with those fellas. Would his girlfriend work with them and look after their overseas interests?

Although Alex preferred not to deal with the possibility, Benny had been playing fast and loose with the truth about the amount of money generated by his ventures compared to the gelt he was sending back east.

If there was a hidden surplus, then Benny may well wish it removed from Vegas so nobody else could get their dirty mitts on it. Geneva would be as good a place as any—these were six and seven-figure sums—as Swiss private bankers asked no impertinent questions like from whom did you steal this money?

But all Alex had at the moment was his belief that something was up—there was no evidence to show Meyer or anyone else from the syndicate. The other issue was whether he wanted to be the fella to rat out Benny. He was one of Meyer's and Charlie's oldest friends— should he really be seen to throw the man to the wolves? Alex met up with Virginia the next day on the pretext of some security matters.

"I'm hoping you'll let me know when you are heading over to Europe again, Virginia."

"This actually isn't any of your business, Alex."

"I agree that what you do is your own affair, but I am responsible for what goes on in Vegas and we believe there are thieves at the airport targeting lone women. We both know you can handle yourself with no help from me, but I would rather be safe than sorry."

"Yesterday you accused me and today you want to be my bodyguard. Why the turnaround?"

"Virginia, let me apologize for the manner I spoke to you then. Part of what I do is to look out for behavior I don't understand or think is unusual. I didn't explain myself to you well enough and came across badly. All I care about is that you and Benny are happy —and you both remain safe."

She looked at him for a while—he was so hard to gauge.

"You were only doing your job, I guess."

"Exactly right. And the best means for me to know you are out of harm's way is if you'll be kind enough to inform me the next occasion you hit the airport. You don't have to say where you are going or why you are heading there, but the date and time of your departure means I can help you between here and the flight."

"Benny is lucky to have a friend like you, Alex."

"You reckon?"

"Too many of the fellas only look after number one. So few understand the bigger picture."

"We live together, we love together, but we die alone."

"That kind of thing, yeah. You guys have a proper sense of camaraderie—I haven't seen that for some time."

"I found that out during the war—those of us who survived did so because we looked out for each other and were damn lucky."

"Benny told me you got a Purple Heart."

"But I did not deserve it. I killed a kid to save a friend, only he was already dead before my shot rang out—big deal."

"I doubt if that's quite what happened. They don't give those things out like candy."

"So you'll let me know your flight plans?"

"Sure, Alex. You've got my back—I understand."

June 1946

30

DESPERATE TIMES CALL for decisive action and Benny had reached the end of his patience with Trans-American.

"We've been scratching away for years, Alex, and I'm sick of fighting with the Nationwide News wire. It's time we dealt with our competition once and for all."

"What are you planning, Benny?"

"James Ragen is on a business trip to the Windy City and we need to ensure he doesn't make it home in one piece."

"He's supported by the Chicago outfit, right?"

"I have syndicate approval for the hit—a majority of the fellas fund us and they want to see an increase in revenue too."

"Have you issued the contract?"

"Not yet, Alex. That's why I wanted to speak with you."

"I don't know anyone who we could call on—my time running Murder Corporation was years ago. My little black book is light of paid killers."

"I wasn't asking you for a recommendation. Instead, you pack a bag and head off to the Windy City this afternoon, Alex."

"Are you sure, Benny?"

"Is there anyone better for the job than you? Get outta here."

ALEX INVITED MASSIMO to join him on the trip and they arrived in Chicago in time for the sun to set over the skyline. They holed up in a cheap hotel—if Alex's life was anything to go by, places like the Hotel Muldrove were only kept solvent through the one-night stays of contract killers. In every city in the land, there were fleapits located close to the station, which were surrounded by low-rent nafkas and guys hooked on brown powder. The Muldrove proved the stereotype.

"Our friend is expected tomorrow morning at an appointment on State Street, so that will be our best opportunity."

The two men made their plans over a simple meal on the edge of the South Side—Alfonse Capone's old stomping ground.

"Tonight we'll boost a car on the north of town and then we can fly by and get the guy, Massimo."

"Works for me. Am I driving or squeezing the trigger?"

"You go behind the wheel—Benny was clear he expected me to do the deed."

Massimo didn't mind either way, he only wanted to know there was a plan to stick to—he was not one to make things up on the spur of the moment. So they waited in a stolen car on East Pershing Road until Alex spotted Ragen's vehicle, just as Benny had described.

Massimo tucked in behind Ragen's black saloon and they carried on south a block until he came to a halt and parked on the right-hand side of the street.

"Steady," warned Alex as he raised the barrel of his rifle to peek out from his window, which he'd wound all the way down. Massimo timed matters perfectly as he pulled up to stop beside Ragen just as the guy hopped out of his car into the road.

Alex fired off three slugs before the racing wire tycoon hit the ground. People screamed and every passerby looked around to figure out where the shots came from and who had been the target for the assault.

Massimo slammed on the gas and they tore away, waiting four blocks before heading back north to the city center and the railway station. Before they got on the train, Alex had the presence of mind to check the late edition and found that Ragen was down but not out.

Somehow the weasel had survived being shot at point-blank range and was being treated for leg and arm wounds at Mercy Hospital.

"Let's get some poison and put this scum out of his misery."

"Alex, you want to take him out from his hospital bed?"

"The longer he's alive, the greater the chance he'll remember details about the car that pulled up alongside him and the faces of the fellas inside the vehicle. We need to get this done tonight."

THREE HOURS LATER and the two men entered Mercy clutching a bunch of flowers each, fedoras clamped as far down at the front of their heads as they could. They both knew the score and Alex kicked off the plan by sauntering up to the reception desk to speak with a nurse behind the counter.

"Sorry to bother you, but I'm looking for a friend of mine. They brought him in earlier today, but I don't know where to find him."

"What's his name?"

"James Ragen."

"He's on the third floor—just ask someone when you get there, but I doubt if they'll let you see him. He is under police guard because of his circumstances."

"Oh no. The least I can do is give him these flowers from me and the fellas. That way, he'll have something to remind him he's not alone."

The nurse feigned interest in Alex's sob story, but she stopped listening almost at the same time as Alex ceased caring about the details of his lie. Up to the third floor and Alex separated from Massimo, who had his own task to complete.

Meanwhile, Alex headed to the desk in the male surgery ward hoping to get close to Ragen. There were cops at the counter and a quick glance showed two officers standing outside a room, which must contain Ragen otherwise what were Chicago's finest doing in the Mercy?

Alex's shoelace mysteriously came loose and he put the flowers down to sort out his shoes. Almost to the second, a loud bang ripped out from the far corridor and the cops in the waiting area raced over to investigate the commotion. Then the two guards ran past and followed their colleagues toward the noise of the blast. Massimo had done well to create such a controlled explosion in the stairwell in such a short amount of time.

In Ragen's room, Alex closed the drapes to hide his activities from any prying eyes. He only had a minute before the cops realized they were chasing a flash in a pan and returned.

The fella was sleeping, so Alex fumbled in his pockets for the syringe and the silvery-white liquid he'd purchased earlier. He didn't need to be that adept with a needle as he poked through Ragen's skin in his upper left arm. Then he plunged the syringe deep inside and squeezed the mercury into the guy's body.

As soon as the spike pierced Ragen's flesh, he woke bolt upright, but Alex placed one palm over the guy's mouth to prevent any sound reaching unsuspecting ears and held him in place while he writhed in agony as the toxic metal took hold. Thirty seconds and he was dead—Alex checked his pulse twice and listened to his heart too.

Five minutes after James Ragen breathed his last, Alex and Massimo met up around the corner and headed to the station.

"You hear about Charlie Lucky, Massimo?"

"What?"

"Dewey commuted his sentence and set him free—only Charlie has had to go home to Palermo."

"Why did that scumbag relent?"

"Charlie helped him during the war on the New York waterfront."

"Stand up fella. Has he had to give up on the syndicate?"

"Not at all, Massimo. He will run things from Sicily."

WITH THE RACING wire king in the ground, Benny and Alex visited the widow within a week of the funeral.

"Mrs. Ragen, we are sorry for your loss and appreciate this is a tough time for you."

Benny was focusing hard on behaving as well as he could, and Alex echoed his manner.

"There is nothing to do to erase the terrible way in which James met his demise, but there is something we can do to ease your anguish over the coming months and years as you learn to live again."

"He was gunned down in the street and then someone walked into the hospital and murdered him in his sleep. What can you offer me to make that pain go away?"

"A million dollars so you will never have to worry about money ever again. It can't bring James back, but it should take the sting out of the day."

The woman eyed Benny suspiciously, but she let him continue—her grief was balanced by the prospect of a sizeable amount of gelt.

"Talk to me about the sting."

"My partner and I would look after the running of the Nationwide News wire that James worked to build up from nothing. That way, you wouldn't have to worry about organizing all those men and the technical equipment, and can find some solace knowing that you will benefit from all of James' hard work. I'm sure that's what he would have wanted."

"Don't be so certain, mister. If you knew my husband as I did, you wouldn't go shooting your mouth off singing his praises. He was a mean, cold-hearted bastard who was only interested in himself and his wealth. He ignored me and the kids from the moment he created that news wire of his. If you're not jerking me around with talk of a million, I'll sign the paperwork right now."

BACK AT EL Rancho, the two men enjoyed a celebratory cocktail.

"Alex, I have a side proposition for you. How hungry are you for the wire?"

"We've spent years trying to build Trans-American up to something and have always been beaten back by those with allegiance to the Nationwide—Jack Dragna and the Chicago outfit. Now we control the only two racing wires in the country, coast to coast."

"Would you like to have it all?"

"What do you mean, Benny?"

"This is the situation. I need to make some payments for the Flamingo and I'm short on gelt, now that Ragen's wife is swimming in small bills. So I'll sell you my fifty percent stake for cash, but I must have the money this week. This is no gentle buyout. You get to dip your beak in every racing bet in America and I have my dream hotel complex."

"How much are we talking?"

"Two million."

Alex whistled through his front teeth.

"I thought Meyer had invested sufficient capital to get the place up-and-running?"

"Don't go concerning yourself about Meyer Lansky and his money. Let's just say we hit some unexpected snags and needed to buy our way out of certain situations. Are you in or not?"

"Mickey and I will own gambling in Nevada and California, and I'll get a percentage of every track bet going. What's not to like?"

"When can I have the gelt?"

"Tomorrow, Benny?"

"Tonight would be better."

Alex shrugged and agreed. He just needed to make a few stops around the outskirts of Vegas to collect his investment capital. He'd been out of the Bowery for longer than he could remember, but he still kept his money in a bunch of holes in crumbling walls.

DECEMBER 1946

31

A BROWN ENVELOPE arrived at Alex's door, shipped special delivery by an unknown courier. Five minutes later, he received a phone call and recognized the voice as soon as the first syllable landed in his ear.

"I sent you a gift. Have you opened it?"

"Yes, I've never had one of those before. How did you know I wanted one?"

"Because you're taking a trip overseas tomorrow and I remember you telling me you didn't need a passport when last you traveled abroad."

"No passports necessary in the American Army."

"A car will pick you up at nine. Be packed and ready to go."

Meyer hung up and Alex was left listening to the buzz at the end of the phone line. He found a case, threw in some clothes, and folded a spare suit on top. Then he had a light supper, watched a show at the Last Frontier, and went to bed early.

His limousine arrived on time the next morning and took him to the airport and within minutes, Alex was walking up the steps into a private plane. Meyer was already sitting inside, reading a newspaper.

"Good to see you. Where are we going?"

Meyer smiled. "To visit Charlie."

"We're off to Sicily?"

"Don't be ridiculous. In this twin prop? He moved to Cuba in October, and he's called a meeting of the syndicate. I think we need you there to hear what you know."

MEYER AND ALEX hotfooted over to the Hotel Nacional de Cuba when they landed in Havana, where Charlie Lucky met them. He gave Alex a massive hug—Alex didn't realize how much he had missed his friend until they were reunited. The three friends headed out to Charlie's residence in Miramar, an area of the city filled with foreign embassies and uptown money.

"So how did Mendy spring you, Charlie? I thought Dewey meant for you to die in prison."

"The special prosecutor wanted my final breath to be the stinking air inside Sing Sing, but he forgot I had connections on the waterfront. During the war, the navy needed eyes and ears focused on any suspicious activities near New York's ports, and I helped."

"In return for an early release?"

"That's right, Alex. Mendy cut me a great deal and then Dewey welched at the last minute and deported me as soon as I stepped outside the prison walls."

"Did any of us ever like that guy? You could never trust him."

"Alex, that man clipped both our wings."

"He still walks free—and they talk as though there's justice in America."

"Listen to the pair of you—calm down and be thankful you both have your health and your wealth."

"Right, Meyer. We live together, we love together…"

"…and we die alone."

The three men nodded and fell to silence. Meyer was right—any fool can complain about his lot. It's what you do with the hand you're dealt that makes the difference between the winners and losers in this world.

"Are you staying a while in Cuba, Charlie?"

"As long as I am able. I like the place—it reminds me of Florida, only in Spanish. Also, I am a handful of miles from America and I can manage the organization easier from here."

"Meyer said there was a meeting planned."

Charlie smiled at how much Alex wanted to be back inside the syndicate.

"That's right. We're inviting you as an advisor which means you will attend and observe all that happens—and make any comments you want, but you have no voting rights."

Alex was close to returning to the inside track, but no cigar.

"And, Charlie, why call the meeting in the first place?"

"I couldn't think of a better excuse to come to Havana and see Frank Sinatra—he's in town this week. Besides, we can hold our discussions without worrying about the cops and the Feds."

THE AGENDA FOR the Havana conference was straightforward— there were only three matters to discuss: heroin trafficking, gambling in Cuba, and the Flamingo. One syndicate member was notable by his absence—Benny Siegel, but apart from that, there were the usual suspects at the Hotel Nacional de Cuba.

Along with Meyer and Charlie were Jack Dragna representing the west coast and a host of fresh faces that Alex didn't recognise. These were the fellas Meyer said were unfamiliar with him and hence reluctant to let him back at the top table, although he was close today. He sat behind Meyer, near enough to lean in and offer private advice where necessary.

"Thank you all for coming to visit me here in my home from home. It ain't Little Italy, but it'll do. While I may have stepped down from running the syndicate when I was in prison, there is still an alignment of interests sitting in this room."

Charlie eyed the attendees one by one—Joe Adonis, Albert Anastasia, and Vito Genovese, along with at least half a dozen others from New York, Anthony Accardo from Chicago, and gang bosses from New Orleans, Buffalo, New Jersey, and Cleveland. Alex looked out at the sea of strangers and returned his gaze to one man:

Anastasia, who didn't even offer him a flicker of recognition. This was the fella who had stolen Alex's drug operation from under him before he visited Sing Sing. All water under the bridge, apparently.

"I have set up supply lines from Africa and South America to guarantee a free flow of heroin into the US."

The men spent the rest of the day hammering out who would get what percentage from the narcotics supplies until everybody was content with their cut. That night the entire group had front row seats at a Sinatra show which took place in the hotel. Meyer explained how he had asked the singer over as a special favor and they all agreed the guy had a voice on him.

THE NEXT DAY, Meyer whizzed through a discussion on some investment plans he'd unearthed in Cuba.

"I am an indirect joint owner of this hotel with President Batista—he's a man who cares for his people but is more interested in the dark art of making money and I hope to work with him as we open up gambling opportunities in this country."

"We all know Meyer has a sharp eye for a deal and the joint we're sitting in is ripe for growth, which is why I invested a hundred and fifty yesterday in the place."

"Thank you for your vote of confidence, Charlie. Just as we have reached into Nevada and California, thanks to Jack and Benny, Batista wants to attract tourists to this island and sees casinos as a way of achieving this goal. He runs his country with an iron fist so the good news is that whatever he wants, he gets."

"And how long do you think he'll maintain his interest in gaming?"

"Albert, I have spent the last two years working with this man and I can guarantee one thing—while the money flows, he will remain interested because he ensures he lines his pockets as well as the vaults of his treasury."

While all these matters had been of mild interest to Alex, there was no need for him to be in the room. Meyer had been kind to invite him, and the fact the others allowed him in showed his star was rising. The next day, he discovered the real reason he was sitting in this room in a luxury hotel in the middle of Havana.

EVERYBODY SAT DOWN with their coffees and Charlie opened the third day of discussions.

"The last item for the meeting is Las Vegas. Talk us through the situation, Meyer."

"Thanks, Charlie. We have four million invested in the Flamingo being built by Benny Siegel. The hotel-casino will open later this week and several of you have expressed concerns about the size of the investment and when we are likely to receive a return."

Every man nodded and a general murmur spread around the room. Alex had no idea that Vegas was the object of such scrutiny from so important a group of people—he operated as though his little empire in Nevada was of no significance to these fellas, but he was wrong.

"The Flamingo was only meant to cost six hundred thousand—that's what Siegel told us he'd need when we first bought in."

"Albert, when I lent Benny the gelt initially, that is what I believed was happening. When more requests for cash came through, I thought we should all have an opportunity to invest."

Meyer was shrewd enough not to take on all the risk himself, even though he and Benny had been childhood friends.

"Now there are other considerations beyond the money for us to discuss, but first I'd like to ask Alex Cohen's opinion on the situation. He is based in Nevada, running the Trans-American racing wire—and he owns two hotels, so he understands the business thoroughly. What do you think of Benny's handling of the Flamingo?"

Alex grabbed a sip of coffee and lit a cigarette—his moment had arrived.

"I've worked with Benny for years and he has supported me with Trans-American very well and his vision for gambling in Vegas is second to none."

"Alex, we all know how Benny was the first to spot the opportunity for building casinos out west, years before the rest of us.

He claimed all he needed was a pack of cards and some green baize. What we need to hear from you is whether Benny is playing with a straight deck. Be honest here—you are among friends."

Alex looked at Albert—was Meyer right? It had been so long since he trusted Anastasia, he thought he might have forgotten how to do it, the *farbissener* momzer.

"He has chosen his suppliers, sometimes using locals instead of our out-of-town friends. Also, I am unaware of the extent his attention has been taken away from the Flamingo by his girlfriend, Virginia Hill."

"Many of us know Virginia—you need not explain any further in that regard." Meyer glanced at Joe Adonis and then at the Chicago representatives. She had either been in their beds or on their payroll.

"Would you say Benny has invested our money wisely?"

"Meyer, I haven't seen the accounts and I know little about putting up a building."

"Has it ever crossed your mind that there might be a discrepancy between what is spent and what Benny has received?"

Meyer had lifted his own ideas out of his head and dropped them into this meeting.

"The costs Benny mentioned to me do not tally with the expenditure. And if I must talk about another fella's finances behind his back, I am not sure his earnings from his casino investments have been accurately reported to the syndicate. Again, I don't know for certain, but it has crossed my mind."

Silence. Alex's heart raced inside his chest. As the words came tumbling out of his mouth, the men in the room lapped up his every syllable. Once he'd stopped, he felt enormous relief—like he'd needed to share his concerns but had no one near enough to listen until now.

"Thanks, Alex. Does Virginia make any trips out of town?"

"About once a month, maybe. She goes to Europe and comes back lighter than when she flew out."

"Alex, how do you know? That's a very specific claim you're making."

"Charlie, when Virginia first came to town, we didn't hit it off, so I kept a watching eye on her in case I needed to protect Benny's interests. I used plane manifests and confronted her, but she said she was looking after the business of our Chicago friends, so I let it go."

Accardo's eyebrows raised to the roof and Alex saw that she had lied to him. Meyer turned his head to face the syndicate.

"As we discussed earlier, there is some evidence that Benny has been skimming a proportion of our investment into private bank accounts in Geneva. I think he has also been omitting some of his income from the casinos and other operations and has been transporting it to Geneva too, with a little help from Hill."

"You think she knows what he's up to?"

"Joe, she's flying to a bank in a foreign country in a private plane. She knows what she is doing, but we don't know if she is in on the scam or just doing what Benny has asked of her."

"She maintains her own apartment in Los Angeles even though she spends almost all of her time in Vegas," Alex added. "I'm not sure she is as committed to Benny as he'd like her to be."

"Let's take a break and when we come back, we need to decide what we will do about Benjamin Siegel."

Charlie stood up and walked out of the room, followed by Meyer. As Alex had no desire to jaw-jaw with the fellas left, he sauntered out and hoped to catch up with his old friends.

HE REACHED THEM before they left the floor to walk around the block.

"Meyer, I felt as though you knew the answers to the questions aimed at me before I opened my mouth."

"We've had our suspicions for a while, Alex, and I needed you to confirm them in front of the others—or show why we were wrong."

"You could have warned me before we walked into the room."

"Alex, what I wanted was for you to give us an honest account of what you saw and what you believe. The syndicate members were clear they didn't want me to coach you. Benny and I go back a long way."

"What now?"

"That's for the syndicate to decide, Alex."

Back upstairs, there were no speeches before the vote and a unanimous decision in favor of whacking Benny for non-payment of monies.

"Charlie, may I make a simple request?"

"What is it, Meyer?"

"Please let us wait until the Flamingo opens before we carry out the contract. If the hotel is successful, then we could recoup the gelt that has been stolen from us and maybe come to some arrangement with Benny over the whole affair."

"As that is only a matter of days, I can accept the wait."

Albert spoke for all of them. As much as Benny needed punishing, everyone knew the last time the syndicate agreed a hit on one of its own was with Dutch Schultz. Charlie broke the silence.

"Let's see if Benny can turn the Flamingo around. If he does, then we will sit down with him and talk. If not then, Meyer, you'll need to organize the contract—that way we'll know the hit has been carried out without malice. This is just business."

With those words, Charlie glanced at Albert Anastasia, who had always had difficulties with Jewish members of the syndicate; a Sicilian, whose prejudices were shaped in the old country and not in modern America.

That night, they broke bread with Sinatra in a private dining room in the hotel and the following day, Alex returned to the Last Frontier.

32

"ALEX, HOW IS my six million investment doing?"

"Meyer, we're getting there. Everything is complete apart from the hotel rooms, and Benny plans to open after Christmas."

"There should be gold leaf on the walls, the amount this thing has cost us."

"Benny wants it all to be perfect."

"Perfect is good, profitable is better."

When the lobby doors were finally opened at the Flamingo, the casino was ready as was the restaurant, but there were none of the promised hundred and five hotel rooms—the second floor was not safe for customers yet and the third comprised a series of floorboard supports and not much else.

"Why didn't you wait until everything was completed, Benny?"

"Because I need to generate some revenue to keep the syndicate off my back, Alex, and we both know you can run a roulette wheel without offering the johns a bed to sleep in afterward."

"Put like that..."

"It cost me four million to get this joint looking as it does on the first floor." That was another number that Alex couldn't make add up—a two million or more gap between what Benny had spent and what he owed Meyer.

Despite Alex's best efforts to round up some johns, Benny refused to give him any gelt for advertising—not one red cent to send a few girls out onto the street with even a flyer and a willing smile.

So Alex was hardly surprised when nobody appeared in the first hour and only two families rolled in to eat at seven. Benny and his Hollywood friend, George Raft, showed up too. The guy seemed down to earth, unlike many of Benny's showbiz connections, but then Raft had started life in a New York gang.

As soon as he saw the chance, Alex slipped away from Benny, Raft, and Mickey who looked set to drink into the night while the Flamingo staff tried to keep the joint running. The chef couldn't handle the three table orders which had rushed at him all at the same time. Alex attempted to offer some direction and a sense of calm to the paying customers and the waiters alike.

At one point, he leaned against a restaurant wall to find the plasterwork crumbling beneath his shoulder. For a man who had taken so much money, Benny didn't look as though he'd spent it on the Flamingo.

"WE ARE GOING to have to shut the place down, aren't we?"

Benny sat nursing a hangover by the El Rancho pool on the following afternoon. Raft and his entourage had shipped back to Los Angeles, and all was quiet in the hotel complex. Alex sipped a coffee and thought about the Flamingo.

"It's not yet fit for purpose, is it, Benny?"

Alex was right and, although it hurt Benny's ego to close the doors so soon after opening night, it was that or watch the place hemorrhage gelt—Benny needed the builders back in to finish the hotel rooms. Only then would families be able to stay over while the husband played cards and the wife watched a show.

"Is there money in the pot to complete the work?"

"Yes, Alex—we only ran out of time. And I must admit I'm my worst enemy, what with me always demanding excellence and not letting second-best be good enough."

"Perfection is a tough beast to ride." Alex wasn't too sure whether he was being sarcastic because of the crumbling plasterwork the night before, but Benny seemed to be sincere in what he said. Perhaps the fella was throwing him a curveball to take his eye off the financing.

ALEX HAD A quiet word with Gus and Moe. Benny had brought them over to Vegas because they knew how to run a gambling joint and keep the other lines of business running alongside the ordinary johns—their expertise covered prostitution, money laundering, and extortion. The list went on, but he didn't want to blow smoke up their asses too much.

"What do you say, fellas?"

"Alex, you know we are always happy to help, but the Flamingo is Benny's show, not ours. I can't speak for Gus, but I wouldn't feel comfortable stomping all over Benny's shoes without his permission."

"I understand, but I'm not asking you to walk in there and run the joint—just keep an eye on it and offer some friendly advice now and again. I've done my best but I have my hands full running the racing wire. What do you think, Gus?"

"Same as Moe. I won't set foot across the threshold without Benny tipping me the nod—unless it's having a drink at the relaunch party."

"You're a funny guy, you know that?"

"I have my moments."

Alex pondered the situation. These two men were the best hope they had of helping Benny land back on his feet. Although Benny hadn't spoken to Meyer since Charlie sailed to Palermo, the fella was under tremendous scrutiny by the syndicate—given the enormous amount of gelt they'd poured into his dream. The place might have been named after the color of Virginia's cheeks, but Benny would be the one blushing if this venture didn't come good. And soon.

"What would it take for you to visit the building four times a month and help keep Benny on track?"

"A small consideration only."

"Five thousand a week until the place reopens and a bonus of fifty if that happens before Pesach in April."

"Each?"

Alex snorted. "If that'll make the difference, then yes."

MARCH 1947

33

"WE GOT THERE, Alex."

"Well done, Benny. You've made it."

They clinked their champagne glasses as they stood in the Flamingo lobby. A parade of famous, renowned, and rich faces flowed past—Benny had invited some of his Hollywood pals, various syndicate members, and other gang bosses, as well as the well-heeled and well-funded citizens of Nevada and beyond.

Alex nudged Benny as Clark Gable wandered by and nodded in their general direction. "I thought you only knew George Raft."

"That once was true, but I've spent enough time in Los Angeles supplying the film studios with cocaine and skirts to know a few other A-listers."

To reinforce the point, Lana Turner broke away from the group and pecked Benny on the cheek, blew a kiss to Alex, and returned to her conversation with Cesar Romero. In the background, the orchestra played on stage—the auditorium had been converted into a dance floor just for the launch night, and couples were already taking advantage of the Cuban band.

Alex's eyes maintained surveillance around the room, noticing when johns walked up the stairs to where the nafkas were stationed, ready to offer a special experience to select guests later in the night. Mickey Cohen's men provided security, so there would be no disturbance from the ordinary citizens and this was a syndicate-funded party so any fella who wanted to cause trouble would make enemies of the most senior criminals in the country.

"How much did it all cost in the end?"

"Six million."

"And boy does it look as though you spent every single cent?"

"Ever since I was a kid, I dreamed of opening a joint like this, where high rollers can lose their dough at poker while their wives watch a show and have a meal."

"You deserve everything that you get, Benny."

"Thanks, Alex."

WITH THE STARS from the silver screen sipping cocktails, Benny moved further inside—he wasn't expecting any other important guests and had timed matters so that the Hollywood names walked into a buzzing, lively venue. He threw a few words out to the press hounds and then Mickey's guys ushered them off the premises so that everyone could enjoy themselves away from the watchful eyes of the news reporters.

Alex stayed in the lobby a while—he was in no mood for the biggest party of the year and, given the discussions in Havana, he couldn't face spending the night listening to Benny brag his way through into the early hours. Instead, Alex took a walk in the grounds to draw some fresh air into his lungs, hoping to clear his head.

Once you left the frontage and followed the path around the side of the hotel toward an entrance to the pool area, the glitz fell away mighty quickly. The walls were painted, but the concrete of the passage was already beginning to crumble—poor quality materials or roughshod work. Neither was a sign of six million dollars spent on the building, despite Benny's claim.

Alex arrived at a patio area near the pool and a waiter swooped up on him and offered some champagne. Armed with the Californian sparkling wine, he wandered past the guests in search of he didn't know what. He sat down on a diving board because he'd had enough of overhearing snippets of other people's conversations.

On the other side of the pool, he spotted Meyer, who was in deep conversation with Moe and Gus. Each time he spoke, he leaned in, preferring to speak into their ears than announce his thoughts to the world at large. Leaving his glass behind, Alex zigzagged in between the party guests until he arrived at his old friend and the other two.

As he walked up, the three fell into silence for a second and Gus glanced at him, before finishing his sentence in Meyer's ear. Alex couldn't hear a word that was said because of the noise of the band.

"I wasn't too sure if you'd show tonight, Meyer."

"You know me, Alex—I love a good party and we are here to celebrate such success."

"That's you all over, Meyer." Alex's deadpan response made Meyer smile, but soon the accountant in him took over again.

"If you'll excuse me, gentlemen, there's someone here I'd like to introduce to Alex."

Gus and Moe nodded acceptance if not consent, and Meyer led Alex over to the other side of the patio, near the entrance to the dance floor.

"Is Sarah still with you, Meyer?"

"Of course. She is well and wishes you kind thoughts—she assumed we'd meet this evening."

A man in a white tux stood holding hands with a woman in a black cocktail dress. The sparkle in the jewelry around her neck and wrists showed these guys were loaded. Although there was a fixed grin on the woman's part, the man's countenance improved as Meyer walked toward him.

"Senator, let me introduce you to a wonderful friend of mine, Alex Cohen."

They shook hands.

"Alex, this is Senator Merrick Townsend. He represents the good people of Massachusetts."

"Do you come from that state, Merrick?"

"Born and bred. If you ever get the chance to visit, let me know and I will show you the sights. Boston is beautiful in the fall."

"Very kind, Merrick. I shall bear that in mind. Although I've been to the city a few times over the years, no one has been gracious enough to treat me as a tourist."

"I am always happy to help a friend of Meyer's."

"And do you find yourself out in Nevada often?"

"First occasion for my wife, Sylvia, but I have been here twice—for business."

"You should sit at one of our poker tables before you leave. Legal gambling is not something you have back home."

"My constituents would not appreciate my spending time occupied in such habits." Alex didn't like being admonished by this bureaucrat, but he kept his peace, knowing Meyer would only have put them together for a good reason. Townsend touched his elbow and hovered his lips near Alex's head. "Once I've ditched the old girl, I'll join you for a few hands if you can organize a private room."

"No problem. If you don't mind, I might invite some of Meyer's friends to come too—only trusted individuals, you understand?"

"That'd be most enjoyable."

AFTER MIDNIGHT, THE crowds remained, although Alex was still far from being in the humor for the festivities surrounding him. As soon as he was able, he hightailed it over to the second floor ostensibly to check that everything was running smoothly with the nafkas.

He walked down the main corridor and all the doors he passed were shut, which meant they were occupied. Any hotel guests had been placed on the fourth floor, so this showed the girls were being kept busy, earning an excellent hourly rate for Alex, who ran all prostitution in town.

At the far end was a room with its door wide open and Alex stepped inside. He had given strict instructions that this was his space for the night so he would have somewhere to hide from the johns. He sat on the bed and nursed his Scotch.

The sounds of the band and the guests mingling around the hotel permeated through the walls and got inside Alex's head. The jollity of the noise contrasted with the stone-cold fact that Alex missed Rebecca. This life had killed her and had driven Sarah away from him. What did he have to show for it? Piles of cash hidden in the

Vegas and LA area, and not much else. His real friends in America were extradited or dead—apart from one: Meyer remained.

While he'd trusted Benny with his life when he first came to town, now things weren't so simple with the syndicate waiting to decide whether to execute the man for wholesale stealing and the way the fella had behaved toward Rebecca. Alex finished his drink just as a knock resounded from the door.

He checked through the peephole and let the girl in–she was one of the women he'd brought in for the night but he didn't know much about her apart from that.

"The girls said you were on your own and, no disrespect, but I thought I'd check on you to see if you wanted a good time."

He cast a glance up and down her body but absorbed nothing of what he'd seen.

"Sure, come on in."

As he closed the door, she removed what few clothes she was wearing and slipped under the crisp white sheets.

"What's your name?"

"You can call me anything you want in the whole wide world."

"Rebecca, then."

He could afford to spend a few minutes more in this room before he'd have to go downstairs and let Townsend win at cards.

34

THE ADVANTAGE OF running the Trans-American news wire was that nobody batted an eyelid if Alex left town for a day or two for some far-flung corner of the country. The Saratoga racetrack was hardly obscure and was a natural place for Alex to want to visit. Its proximity to Manhattan gave him ample cover to hide the fact his real purpose was to meet up with Meyer Lansky.

Having conquered his fear of flying with his Havana jaunt, Alex took advantage of this newly found transportation option and hopped on a plane to New York so that the trip didn't take forever. Meyer had hired a private room, and Alex only entered when he could be sure all the waiters had left.

"Good to see you, Meyer."

"Likewise, Alex. I'm glad you could pop over at such short notice."

"For you, anything."

Both guys smiled and Alex sipped the Scotch Meyer had ensured was waiting for him on his arrival. There were plates of sandwiches and chips too, in case either of the men became hungry during their conversation. Two pots of coffee were sitting at the ready as well.

"How's life in the syndicate?"

Before Meyer parted his lips, the crowd roared as the next race started and a bunch of thoroughbreds shot along the track with the sole aim of getting past the post before any of the others.

"Same old. You know what it's like. How is Vegas?"

"Quiet. We've soaked up all the racing wire business there is to get in town and Ezra and Massimo spend most of their time on the road, either encouraging new customers to join or collecting subscriptions. Mickey keeps the gambling ticking over and Benny looks like he's turned the corner with the Flamingo."

"Really?"

"He said it had made a quarter of a million, which at its first launch, I never dreamed was possible. The fella appears to have got it together."

"That's good. I'm glad Benny's dream hasn't been for nothing."

"But I doubt if you asked me to fly halfway across the country just to hear what you already know about our activities in Las Vegas."

"You are right, Alex. There is a specific item I need us to discuss."

Another roar as the race reached its conclusion and a rank outsider won, much to most people's annoyance. Alex sat up in his seat, not because of the excitement of what was happening on the track but because of Meyer's words and the serious expression on his face.

"What is it, Meyer?"

"At the end of last year, you watched as the syndicate agreed to hold back on taking action against Benny. I did my best to protect him, but the others have lost patience."

Alex inhaled because he thought he knew what was coming next, but he didn't want to say it out loud in case he was wrong.

"I appreciate the Flamingo has turned a profit, but it is nothing compared to the amount Benny owes us. At this rate, it will be at least two years before we get our money back and, even then, there is the matter of Benny's robbery from his friends."

Alex swallowed, feeling Meyer's pain as he spoke. A sip of coffee eased the dryness in his throat.

"And what have they instructed, Meyer?"

"Charlie has made it clear that the group will proceed with the contract and it's my job to make sure it gets done."

"By your hand?"

Meyer looked out at the race as the horses thundered past, almost as if he couldn't bring himself to answer Alex's question.

"That would be ideal, but I don't think I can do it. He's saved my life too many times over the decades."

"Is that why I'm here?"

"I'd like you to take on the contract, yes."

"You want me to kill Benny Siegel?"

"That's what I'm asking. Will you?"

He nodded his consent—he had been the one to hit Dutch Schultz all those years ago, but that didn't make it any easier. His relationship with Benny was different—they had spent so much time together, working closely in Vegas and New York before.

June 1947

35

"HOW HAVE YOU been, Virginia?"

Alex and Hill had spent little time in each other's company and hadn't been in the same room together since the opening night of the Flamingo. He had eased off his dislike of her when he realized she was only doing Benny's bidding—knowingly or otherwise. Once that idea had permeated his mind, Virginia diminished in Alex's esteem but he was more sympathetic to her situation.

"Not so bad, Alex. Life keeping you busy?"

"As ever. There's always someone to see—the race wire business doesn't run itself."

"I suppose not." She looked around the Flamingo bar area, in search of Benny, but he wasn't there.

"Drink?"

"A cosmo would be most pleasant."

They passed the time of day amicably enough for a few minutes and then lapsed into silence. The only thing they had in common was Benny, and that didn't stretch conversation beyond an initial hello. They sipped their cocktails and Alex inquired about LA.

"Do you still keep that apartment in Malibu?"

"Beverly Hills," she corrected him. "Yes."

"I'd like to entertain a guest somewhere discreet but homely. Are you planning one of your trips soon?"

Virginia eyed him suspiciously.

"That's not an issue—you want my place for how long?"

"Only a night. Maybe two."

"You often meet business acquaintances of an evening in an apartment? Alex, I thought you men used bars and backroom gambling dens to talk over work."

"Who said anything about business?"

Virginia smiled and touched his arm briefly before taking another sip of her cosmo.

"You can't fool me, Alex. If there was a woman involved, then you wouldn't want me to know about it and you'd hire some suite—with a better view of the beach."

"The reason isn't that important—I just would prefer to go somewhere discreet and not one of our usual haunts. The guy is from out of town and I'd like to set him at his ease. He thinks it is dangerous to hang out with men like me."

"You expect me to believe that?"

"It's the best answer on offer."

She looked at him again and decided.

"I hope she's worth it. Yes, you can have my apartment."

"Will you be out of town in a week or so, do you expect?"

"While you won't admit to having a girlfriend, I'll tell you I'm planning a trip to France. I might not have told you before, but I am seeing a guy there."

"Hence all your flights to Europe?"

"Pretty much."

"What does Benny think of the situation?"

"He has his wife, I have my man in Paris. And because he's in another country, there will never be a time when he and Benny cross paths."

"You've got it all worked out."

Her story didn't chime with what Meyer said was going on, but at least she would be out of the way.

"I will let the super know to expect you once we've confirmed the dates and I'll leave a key for you with him."

"Perfect. When did you say you were off?"

"I didn't, Alex—Guillaume is waiting for me to arrive so I can leave whenever suits."

"How about Monday?"

"That'll give me the weekend to get ready."

"Just make sure you're flying on Monday."

Perhaps Virginia noticed the change in Alex's tone, or maybe she caught a hint that he wanted her out of the country. Either way, that Monday Virginia Hill stepped onto Benny's private plane and flew to Paris. If Guillaume was a fictitious character, it didn't matter to Alex. The guy was as real as Virginia needed him to be and the LA apartment was secured.

36

MONDAY LUNCHTIME, ALEX arrived at the outskirts of the City of Angels and entered a diner for a bite to eat. His rental car contained an overnight bag with three changes of clothing, a case containing a pool cue, and a pack of playing cards.

He spent the next two nights in a motel near Long Beach, only stepping outside to grab some food, never going to the same place twice. Alex read the LA newspaper, made some calls to Ezra and Massimo to ensure that business was running smoothly, and played numerous games of solitaire.

On Wednesday, Alex swapped his rental for a local automobile and drove over to Beverly Hills, where he settled in an apartment with a clear line of sight onto Virginia's home. He unpacked his clothes, hung them in a wardrobe, and placed his playing cards on a coffee table in the living room. Then he went back to the car and drove to Fairfax, where he met Jimmy the Hawk in a pool hall.

Jimmy was one of those characters you saw on the other side of a joint and knew to avoid. It wasn't his appalling body odor, although he suffered from that affliction no matter how many times he showered. And it wasn't his gruff manner which annoyed people almost before they began speaking with him.

Jimmy's nickname was a clue—due to an accident while street fighting as a kid, his right eye was not pointing in the usual direction, the eyeball having been twisted out of its normal countenance. So his face was distorted in a way that made women avert their gaze and men wonder whether or not they were being stared at. Alex knew him as one of the most reliable fellas for firearms, and that was the purpose of his visit.

He spotted Jimmy sat at the bar near the entrance and stood by until the one good eye noticed him. They walked to the rear and found a table away from any other customer. Alex ordered a coffee and Jimmy got another beer.

"Thanks for meeting me, Jimmy."

"Always glad to help a friend, but are you certain you want anything from me at all? You look like you're only here for a game."

Alex looked down at his cue case and smiled.

"This is for you or one of your guys to play with until the end of the week. Make certain it gets used as it's brand new so any marks they produce will stand out well."

"Understood. I'll give it to the worst player I know."

"Fine but it needs to be returned and still be usable. If anyone were ever to ask, this is evidence to corroborate my alibi."

"I get it. And I assume you are seeking something in exchange?"

"That was what we agreed. Have there been any issues with my requirements?"

"No, Alex. I would have preferred more time to acquire the principal item, but we both know that I factored difficulty into the price."

"It is what it is. Before you hand the cue over to your lunk, check the lining of the case and the gelt will be there as requested."

"Too kind, Alex."

"Where are the goods?"

"In the trunk of my car, which is parked in the lot."

"Finish your beer and then we can close out our arrangement."

They spent the next five minutes in small talk as Alex watched the contents of Jimmy's glass drain away. Once the last vestige of amber liquid journeyed down the guy's throat, Alex took a swig to finish his coffee and the two left the building.

Alex drove up to Jimmy's vehicle and in a twinkle of an eye, a bag was removed from one car and deposited in the other's trunk. They shook hands and Alex sped away with the promise of dropping

Jimmy a dime when he wanted his cue back, probably Friday but by Saturday at the latest.

HIS BEVERLY HILLS pad was better appointed than the first fleapit he'd landed in. There were two bedrooms and the living area had more space. There was a coffee pot in the kitchen and that was all Alex wanted for cooking. Best of all was the view.

The living quarters possessed a glass wall that led onto the balcony, and even if you didn't step outside, you could still see forever. Or rather, with a scope sight clamped to your eye, Alex had a direct line into Virginia's apartment.

He set up the tripod supplied by Jimmy right by the balcony entrance so if he opened the double doors, the barrel of his semi-automatic wouldn't need to stick out of the building in view of prying neighbors, but Alex could still get a clean shot. Until it was needed, he kept the firearm in its case, only taking it out to check the mechanism.

Today was only Wednesday, and Meyer would place the call to Benny tomorrow and arrange to meet him on Friday. Alex had plenty of time to kill. He whipped out his playing cards, put on a pot of coffee, and settled in for a long wait.

ALEX WOKE UP on Thursday to discover himself still lying on the couch, but he shook himself together and took a shower to wash the cobwebs away. He popped down to a diner five blocks from the apartment for breakfast and visited a general store on the way to grab some snacks and buy more coffee.

Back in his lair, he hunkered down, played cards, and stared out of the window. His life in Vegas had been mixed. While he had made more money than he had ever known in New York, he had found and then lost Rebecca. In between, Benny had gotten fresh with her and Alex'd done nothing in retaliation. Although he hadn't told himself this, Alex had never forgiven himself for that lack of action—

it was so unlike him. Sometimes he wondered who he was. Some jumped-up *lobus*—all words and no deeds?

He stood on the balcony and stared out at the anonymous panorama in front of him. Los Angeles was a sprawling mass of humanity, but with no heart. Every other place he had been in, Alex knew where the city center was, but not here. It was just a set of jigsaw pieces with no picture. That night he made sure he slept in a bed so he'd be able to come out all guns blazing the following day.

AFTER BREAKFAST IN a different diner in the other direction from the apartment, he went to a pay phone and called New York.

"It's me." Alex relied on Meyer recognizing his voice.

"Hi. All good?"

"At my end, yes. Did you make the arrangements?"

"I did."

"When?"

"Today. At the time we discussed."

"Good. I'll speak later when everything has happened."

"Thank you."

Alex checked his watch in reflex–he had hours before his quarry would be in Virginia's place, so he went home and waited some more.

THAT EVENING, HE removed the M1 carbine from its case and propped it up on the tripod. With the drapes drawn, nobody casting an eye toward his balcony would see anything to make them concerned. Alex had instructed Jimmy to modify the rifle so that a scope was mounted on the top. This had cost a considerable penny, but Alex wasn't a kid any more and being a sniper was a young man's game. Anything to give him an edge was most welcome.

As the light faded, Alex used his scope to check on Benny's arrival. Meyer had called him and asked for a private meeting in Los Angeles. Knowing Virginia was out of town, Benny suggested her place as a safe, discreet location—as predicted. They had agreed that Meyer would show at ten and that he'd explain everything when they were in the same room, but it was a tremendous business opportunity.

What Alex did not expect was for Benny to appear with another man. He didn't recognize the fella, but judging by their body language, they knew each other well. Maybe Benny wanted to hook this guy up with Meyer as an extra investor. Whatever the reason for bringing a stranger to a private meeting, this would add complications to what he needed to do.

Virginia's living room comprised a long three-seater couch with two armchairs opposite, separated by a low coffee table. On the sideboard on the left was a radio set next to a cocktail cabinet. Judging by Benny's frequent trips, it was well stocked.

At the allotted hour, Benny sat at one end of the couch which faced the window, and the other man perched in the direct line of fire between the muzzle of the rifle and Benny. Why was the guy even in the room? There was no time for Alex to consider this question because the minutes were ticking away and Benny would only stay for a while before he got impatient with Meyer's no-show and stormed off.

Alex stood with the butt of the rifle wedged into his shoulder. As he put his finger on the trigger, readying himself for action, Alex felt the rifle shaking in his hands. Was he going to be able to kill his friend? All his other hits had been strangers, more or less. Then a memory of Rebecca's torn blue dress lying on the cottage floor flitted through his mind and Alex exhaled and gripped the rifle once more.

Fat Max refused to do anything but sit in his chair and stare at Benny, who would pop up out of his seat to grab another drink and scurry back. Alex needed more time for a clean shot. He took three deep breaths to calm himself down and stared back into Virginia's apartment. Fat Max was sitting down and passing a newspaper over to Benny. Damn—a golden opportunity missed.

Max tapped at a particular story he wanted Benny to read, and as he leaned forward in his chair, Benny's entire body became visible. Alex put his finger on the trigger and squeezed off a shot that passed through Benny's right cheek and out of the left-hand side of his neck.

Blood poured out and Max spun round, having whipped out a pistol. Then Alex released a second slug that caught Benny in between his nose and right eye. His body remained pinned to the couch as more red pulsed out of the fella's head. All this time, Max stood and swiveled around hoping to find the assailant.

To ensure he didn't have another James Ragen on his hands, Alex fired off several more bullets into Benny's body—one way or another that man would not survive this assassination. Then he aimed the rifle at Max who continued to face the window and, for a moment, it felt to Alex like the guy saw straight into his balcony. He considered dispatching Fat Max but decided against it—he was a witness who had seen nothing and wasn't worth killing.

Alex closed the drapes, packed the rifle away, sat back on the couch, and lit a cigarette. Before he inhaled his second puff, Alex sobbed and then he cried, muffling his mouth with both his hands.

He had murdered his friend and was no better than any of the street scum he had spent his life trying to rise above. What's more, the syndicate viewed him as only a gun for hire and he would never return to the top table.

And then there was Rebecca. She was gone for good and it was only now that Alex allowed the empty gnawing in the pit of his belly to ooze out of his eyeballs in salty tears. His thoughts raced on and arrived at Sarah. Why had he been so stupid for so many years when he had the chance for happiness? Alex was alone in the world with only one friend whom he'd seen a mere handful of times in the past decade.

He pulled himself together, emptied the apartment of any personal items, and headed to his car. Although he had told Jimmy he would return the rifle, Alex knew this would never happen, which was why he had agreed to Jimmy the Hawk's ridiculously high price.

He drove around the city, stopping to throw pieces of the now-destroyed firearm into various dumpsters across town. Then he dropped a dime.

"There's been a change of plan, Jimmy. You can keep the cue as I can't trade your item back."

"I thought you might say that. Did everything work out for you?"

"Peachy."

At a different phone booth, Alex called Meyer to utter one sentence.

"It's done."

"Thank you."

Then he settled into his rental and drove all the way home, stopping only once to freshen up and grab a coffee and a piece of cheesecake.

37

ALEX FLOPPED INTO his bed at the Last Frontier and grabbed three hours sleep before he had to wake up and face the dawn. He found he was still wearing the clothes he'd had on when he murdered Benny Siegel, so he hopped into the shower and threw his sweat-encrusted shirt into the trash. Then he called down to housekeeping for them to get his suit cleaned and pressed and settled into his day.

Under these circumstances, routine is everything and although he wanted to eat in his room, Alex forced himself to go to the hotel restaurant as he did every other morning he was in town.

The newshounds had been busy while he was driving back from LA because the lead headline declared Benny was dead, killed by an unknown assassin. The second paragraph claimed he'd been shot in the eye, but that wasn't true—you can't believe everything you read.

Some people took a different approach to their newsgathering and accepted every word as solid. Mickey Cohen stormed into the restaurant clutching a copy of the paper and threw it down on Alex's table, only just missing his coffee and juice.

"Have you seen this?"

He stabbed a finger at the headline, which was identical to the one in Alex's hand; he placed the newspaper on top of Mickey's to emphasize the point. Before Alex answered, Mickey replied for him.

"Someone's done for Benny."

"You know who?"

"What're you trying to say? Of course, I don't know the trigger man. How about you?"

"No clue, Mickey."

"I thought you were tight with all your syndicate pals."

"Mickey. From the moment I went inside, I've been waiting to get back to the top table, but they don't want me. So, no, I have no idea who whacked Benny and if it was a Murder Corporation hit, then they didn't bother to ask my permission first, despite what you may think."

"I'll put a contract out on whichever scumbag did this."

"Even if it was sanctioned by the syndicate?"

Mickey thought for a minute because Alex had asked a good question. The fella might have red mist in front of his eyes—the ex-boxer in him meant he was a fighter and a survivor—but he didn't intend to get on the wrong side of the men who ran America's organized gangs.

"I will kill the *pishers* who did for Benny but then I'll leave it there. I've no beef with the fellas in charge."

A waiter hustled toward Mickey and asked if he was available to take a phone call.

"Who is it?"

"The gentleman preferred not to give his name, but he insisted I find you and that you'd be interested in the information he has to offer."

Mickey tutted and followed the guy out, returning two minutes later.

"A connection says the momzers are hiding in the Hotel Roosevelt."

"They capped Benny and had time to get over here?"

"If they drove all night, they could have."

"I guess…"

"I'm going over to make some inquiries."

"Mind if I tag along? We might not always see eye-to-eye, Mickey, but Benny was my friend too."

A nod from the squat man seething before him and Alex swigged back his coffee and followed Mickey out and over to the Roosevelt.

BY THE TIME Alex arrived at the hotel, Mickey's sedan had halted at an angle in front of the main reception entrance and the driver's door was wide open. He ran inside before Mickey did anything stupid. Alex knew for sure that whoever Mickey was gunning for was as innocent as the day they were born—and might not deserve to be killed by him based on the testimony of some guy's phone call.

As Alex stood in the lobby looking around, Mickey pulled out two handguns and fired several times into the ceiling. "The guys who whacked Benny Siegel have ten minutes to come outside to account to me for their actions." Then he stormed out and paced up and down by his car.

Alex glanced at his watch and leaned against Mickey's sedan while the two men waited for the non-existent guests to leave their rooms and volunteer to be shot down by Mickey Cohen. This was not a brilliant plan by anybody's standards.

Fifteen minutes later and even Mickey was sensing that it wasn't working, especially when they heard police sirens in the distance.

"We need to get out of here, Mickey. The last thing either of us needs is to have to explain to the cops why you were shooting indiscriminately in the hotel lobby, shouting about Benny Siegel."

Mickey glanced at the road and then fixed his gaze on Alex.

"Yeah, let's get outta here."

AS THEY DROVE out of the parking lot, Mickey turned left and zoomed down the highway. In contrast, Alex went right and paid a visit to the Flamingo as Meyer's investment was leaderless.

When he arrived, Alex found Ted Bean, the manager.

"Judging by the downbeat mood, you've all heard about Benny?"

"Yes, it is so shocking."

"It sure is. The trick is to keep going. Take every day as it comes, but the Flamingo was Benny's dream and there is no way he would want the place to go to hell just because he wasn't around to look after it."

"I told the staff the same thing, Alex. And at some point, once all the furor dies down, we will find out who our new owners are. Someone is bound to buy up his stake, right?"

"You can be sure of that, Ted."

A call came through from reception that two men were asking for Bean. Alex accompanied him back to the lobby and found Moe and Gus waiting.

"Good to see you. You heard the news, right?"

"Yes, Alex, that's why we're here."

"Oh?"

"We're looking after the place now."

Meyer hadn't wasted a minute before installing his new management. Ted Bean might have the job title, but the decisions would be made by Meyer's men.

"Congratulations. Couldn't have happened to a nicer pair of fellas."

Benny was dead, the Flamingo was in safe hands and the syndicate would control its most expensive asset until it had rung the place dry of gelt. Alex was left back where he had been—running prostitution in Vegas and the racing wire across the country for Meyer and the boys out east.

38

"THERE IS A tough choice to be made, Alex, and that is why I dragged you down from Vegas."

Meyer and Alex sat in a pair of casual dining chairs on a patio area overlooking South Beach in Miami. Meyer had explained during their brief phone call that he was spending much of his time at present in Cuba and that Miami would be a convenient location for them to meet up.

Alex didn't mind too much where they held their discussion. While Moe and Gus were running the Flamingo—and doing well by all accounts—there was the bigger picture to focus on.

"We need someone to oversee Las Vegas for us, Alex, and there are three names we are looking at. Jack Dragna, Mickey Cohen, and you."

Meyer sipped his coffee and stirred in a small amount of sugar.

"Dragna has wanted a piece of Vegas ever since Benny first headed west in search of his gambling fortune."

"The guy is hungry for it and competent."

"Would you say the same of Mickey?"

Meyer smiled. "What do you think of the fella? You've seen him operate the last few years."

"To be honest, there's too much of the boxer still in him. He is quick to temper and acts before he thinks through the consequences."

"So your money would be on Dragna?"

"If it were a two-horse race, yes. But that says less about Jack and more about Mickey's shortcomings as a leader."

"The tension in your voice implies there is some bad blood between you."

"Meyer, we had a few run-ins, mainly over Trans-American."

"That must be all in the past though, right?"

"If you are asking me whether I could work with him then, yes, I would suck in my animosity toward him for the greater good."

"Did things get that bad?"

"We had our moments, but that is all water under the bridge."

"Alex, whoever gets the job will need to be trusted—after Benny's thieving hands, the syndicate is concerned that all and any tribute winds up in their pockets."

"You know what happened to Virginia Hill? I haven't seen her in town since Benny's demise."

"She won't be coming round Vegas soon."

"Was there a contract?"

"Oh no, nothing of the sort. I just meant that without her sugar daddy, she will seek some other fella to nest near. She's a nafka in all but name."

"Harsh. She only ever had one john in play at a time."

"Says who?"

Meyer's question stunned Alex—he had always assumed that the woman was soaking Benny for all he was worth, and that was all. He had never considered that she might have several men in tow around the country—or that her story about a French lover was anything but a tissue of lies.

"Meyer, did anyone pay to clean her apartment?"

THE CONVERSATION CARRIED on over dinner. His friend found the perfect venue—a restaurant that served Italian-Yiddish cuisine, just like being back in Midtown during Prohibition. By the time they'd consumed the last cannoli, Alex wasn't sure he had any space for the cheesecake, which Meyer assured him was to die for.

As they savored their coffees, Meyer returned to the earlier topic.

"As I was saying, we are down to three candidates for the Vegas job."

"Am I still in the running?"

"What makes you think you've dropped off the list since this morning?"

Alex considered a minute–if they were going to hand Vegas over to Jack Dragna, then Meyer wouldn't have made a special trip over to Florida or got him to fly down from Nevada.

"We spent all the time talking about Jack and Mickey, I assumed I was out."

"There is a world of difference between discussing your competition and losing the race, Alex."

"To be honest, if you give the place over to the ex-boxer then I will leave town and never come back. I don't mean to be dramatic, but the guy is a flake."

"He was always Benny's man, not mine."

"If I wanted somebody to organize security or run a team of killers, then Mickey would be the fella I'd call."

"For sure. So that leaves you and Dragna."

Alex frowned at the same time as Meyer smiled.

"I've been messing with you, Alex. There's wonderful news and some not so good news—which would you like first?"

"Always the bad news, Meyer. What gives?"

"You are not yet a member of the syndicate. There remains a whiff of concern about trust from some newer members. I know and you know that it is nonsense—they believe the rumors about you from before you did your time. Whatever the basis, that is the decision."

"Well, that's a punch in the belly. What's the good news?"

"We want you to run Las Vegas for us. You report to me. Congratulations."

November 1950

39

MENDY GREENBERG HIT town two days before Alex was to appear in front of the Kefauver committee hearings in Las Vegas. He had been Alex's lawyer when Dewey took him down and had been Charlie Lucky's advocate too.

"I haven't seen you for a lifetime—you're clearly keeping out of trouble."

"Mendy, I have spent my career trying to keep my nose clean— and once you have been in prison, you know how important it is to never go back."

"It must have been hard, but you've done well since you got out, so Meyer's told me."

"We had some tough rides, but now that Trans-American is ticking over, I can keep an eye on my other interests."

"No need to be coy with me, Alex. We have client-attorney privilege to protect us."

"Mendy, forgive me but I'd rather not talk as though I dip my beak into every piece of action in the city, but there isn't a nafka on her back or a bet being placed that I don't receive some appreciation for. If a union official sneezes out of turn, I get paid."

"How's the hotel business?"

"You ask even though you know already. Benny was right—the Flamingo's been a superb model and the syndicate has made several investments in the casinos here. It is a license to print gelt and also, with so much cash floating around, money laundering becomes a cinch for our other operations."

THE TELEVISION CAMERAS turned to face Alex in the committee room as he returned to his chair after taking his oath to tell the truth, the whole truth, and not to deviate from that plan of action at any point in the proceedings.

Estes Kefauver was enjoying all the new media attention because smugness oozed out of every pore–each time the cameras trained their lenses on him, he sat up ever so slightly straighter.

"Let's keep this simple, shall we, gentlemen?"

Alex stared at this man from Tennessee with his track record of cleaning up malpractice and wrongdoing wherever he went. This was no Thomas Dewey hoping to make a career—this guy already had juice.

"Mr. Cohen, let me remind you, you are under oath. Are you, or have you ever been, an active participant in the organized crime syndicate known as the mafia?"

"No, I have never been a member of the mafia."

Mendy leaned over to Alex and covered the mike with his hand. Ten seconds whispering in his ear and Alex continued.

"While the senator might wish to rush through proceedings, besmirching people's good names as he goes, I would like to remind this committee I am a hard-working immigrant, who owns a service used by millions of law-abiding citizens every day. I appear before you of my own volition."

"Thank you for the edited highlights of your life, Mr. Cohen, but you have omitted to mention that you served jail time for federal tax evasion."

"Everybody makes bad choices at some point—mine was not to keep good paperwork. I haven't made that mistake again. Have you performed any errors of judgment over the years, Senator Kefauver?"

"You are here to answer my questions and not the other way around, Mr. Cohen."

"Then ask your questions—I will help as best I am able."

"Did you know Arnold Rothstein?"

"Yes, I met a fella of that name, but he died over twenty years ago."

"Do you, or did you, know a man named Charles Luciano?"

"Again, there was a guy who left the country a decade ago with that name with whom I was acquainted."

"And how about Bugsy Siegel?"

"I knew a Benjamin Siegel, but not this bug you talk about, although call an exterminator as there are cockroaches all over this room."

The onlookers behind Alex laughed, but he didn't turn around and kept his gaze on the man in front of him. Mendy leaned in again.

"Don't get too fresh with this guy. He tears men limb from limb if he chooses."

"The committee appreciates your concern for its health and the environment in which it operates. Cockroaches are attracted to utter filth and we are in Las Vegas."

Alex smiled and kept schtum, following Mendy's advice.

"Mr. Cohen, Benjamin Siegel is dead, is he not?"

"This is true."

"Your colleagues are dead or deported. You admit you consort with criminals?"

"All I told you was that I knew people of the same name as the individuals you mentioned. That does not mean I was friends with any of them, Senator."

"But the man sat next to you was Luciano's counsel until the felon was sent back to Sicily. Are you telling this committee that you only knew a man of the same name as Charles Luciano?"

Alex inhaled as he prepared to answer the direct question, but he was interrupted by Merrick Townsend, sat to Kefauver's right.

"Senator, forgive me, but I must leave shortly on some Massachusetts business. Before I go, I wanted to put on the record that I have known Alex Cohen for several years personally and have found him to be nothing other than polite, charming, friendly, and the epitome of the American way. This is a man who came to this country with only the clothes on his back and is now responsible for

Trans-American, a nationwide news service, used by many God-fearing and taxpaying citizens every day of their lives."

Kefauver stared at Townsend as he stood up and walked out of the room. Alex made a mental note to comp the senator an extra nafka when he came to town next. Then Kefauver continued as though the interruption had not happened.

"As I was saying, Mr. Cohen, do you not know Lucky Luciano?"

"Senator, my belief was that you were interested in rooting out the contagion of crime that has blighted this land ever since the Pilgrim Fathers stole turkeys the first winter after they arrived. From what I have read in the papers, Mr. Luciano is no longer living here and therefore can have nothing to do with any criminal activities which may or may not take place here."

"Answer my question."

"I will respond to any accusations you wish to make about crimes that have occurred but I do not see any value in confirming whether I know some men who are dead or gone from this country. The viewing public expects more from their elected officials, I would imagine."

Kefauver looked at the cameras then flitted his attention to Alex. Then back to the cameras with their red lights shining out, and on to Alex again.

"Mr. Cohen, if you don't change your attitude, I will hold you in contempt."

Mendy took this opportunity to speak.

"May I remind this committee that my client has come here of his own free will and has said he is prepared to subject himself to your questioning. There is no contempt here—only a genuine interest in furthering the aims of this board as it investigates crime."

"Then get him to answer my query."

"Senator, tell me what the question was and I will gladly respond."

"Do you know Charles Luciano?"

"As I have already told you, I used to know him before he left for Sicily. Your question is designed so I cannot give you a straight answer. It is almost as if you want to make me appear evasive in front of this committee."

"Why would I want to do that, Mr. Cohen?"

"Yet another question I can't possibly answer. I repeat that I will gladly help you eradicate criminals from our cities and towns, but you sound more like a country bumpkin on a fishing trip. Do you have anything specific about any crimes that have been committed that you want to ask me about?"

"Your impertinence is noted, Mr. Cohen, and at this time I will not be presenting any evidence to the committee of particular criminal malfeasance. The purpose of these hearings is to paint a picture of how crimes are taking place across this great nation, which is controlled by a group of key individuals known as the mafia."

"And I have already told you I am not, nor have ever been, a member of the mafia. Senator, if there is nothing else of any substance you will add then the American taxpayer deserves to hear from a different voice because you've finished flogging this dead horse."

Alex stood up and walked out of the room, almost before Mendy grabbed his papers and followed him out. As soon as he exited the courtroom, light bulbs popped around him as the reporters grabbed a photo before hitting him with a barrage of questions he refused to answer.

When he got into the sedan positioned for him out front, Alex waited for Mendy to catch up and then Ezra drove the vehicle away at high speed before any press car followed them back to the Last Frontier.

40

"I SAW YOUR performance on the television, Alex. You did very well. Congratulations."

"Thank you, Meyer. I'm glad to hear you were watching—the last time I was in court, nobody was there to support me, apart from Mendy here."

The three men chuckled and sipped at their drinks; Alex had chosen his usual Scotch on the rocks.

"Did you think I appeared too aggressive? The pinhead rankled me—I didn't want to react, but I couldn't leave it alone either."

"I've spoken with the fellas back east, Alex, and they were mighty impressed with the way you handled yourself. Mendy, I think you need to make a phone call, right?"

"Sure, Meyer."

The lawyer set off to walk around the block as he didn't fancy pretending to speak on a phone while his clients held a private meeting. Meyer waited for Mendy to be out of sight before continuing.

"First, you were not alone in court when Dewey took you down for tax evasion. How do you think your sentence was kept short? I made a payment to your judge's benevolent fund."

"I never knew. Thank you, old friend."

"Second, the syndicate members have been talking about you. I have been pleading your case for years, as you know, and I reached a deal with them last month—depending on how you did today. Alex, I can't tell you how happy I am to invite you into the syndicate again. You will have full voting rights from now on. Welcome back."

Alex squeezed his tumbler until, realizing it might shatter, he released his grip. His words caught in his throat and all he could do was nod in acceptance. Meyer put a hand on his friend's arm as Alex wiped away a solitary tear from his left eye. Five minutes later, Mendy returned and hovered in the periphery of Alex's vision until Meyer beckoned for him to sit down.

"Mendy, we have something to celebrate—Alex just got a promotion. Does the Last Frontier stock any French champagne, Alex?"

A SECOND BOTTLE of bubbly later, Meyer suggested they go out to eat instead of staying at the Frontier all evening.

"I got the concierge to book us a poolside table at El Rancho—I know how much time you spent there before you had this place to run, Alex."

Massimo drove them the few blocks to Benny's first hotel investment in Vegas, and Alex recalled those early days when Meyer dragged him over from LA to work with Benny and build up business in this desert town.

The maître d' took them to the table Alex knew only too well, but there was already somebody sat there. Meyer waved as they approached, and it took Alex a minute to recognize the fourth guest —Sarah. Alex's face formed a query.

"I brought my executive assistant with me as we have business to discuss tomorrow. Do you mind that I invited her for dinner?"

"Not at all."

As they arrived at the table, she stood and beamed, heading straight for Alex to give him a kiss on the lips. Then she shook hands with Mendy—the way they smiled at each other showed they had met before.

"How are you, Sarah?"

"All the better for seeing you, Alex."

◆ ◆ ◆

AFTER DINNER, MEYER and Mendy made their excuses and left while Alex and Sarah finished a bottle of red.

"Sarah, you know I hadn't turned my back on you and the boys, but the work I was doing was dangerous and I didn't want to repeat past mistakes."

"Meyer's been keeping me up-to-date with your exploits. After Benny died, I thought you might have reached out then."

"At that point, it felt too long and I wasn't sure you'd have wanted me to show up, anyway. How are the boys?"

"The men have all flown the coop—I've missed you, Alex Cohen."

"Straight back at ya. It's been a lonely few years…"

Sarah nodded as Alex's voice trailed off and he thought about Rebecca, recalling the moment when she died.

"I told you I ended it with my lawyer guy, Kameron? Not everyone behaves as well as you."

"If I had known then, you wouldn't have had any trouble from him. You mentioned he was just remote. You should have said."

"Alex, a woman can't run to her ex-husband every time her current boyfriend lays a hand on her."

He ground his molars as he imagined somebody harming his Sarah.

"Did that go on for long?"

"First time I put it down to his drinking. The second, I threw him out. When he tried to return, two of Meyer's colleagues discussed matters with him and I have never seen him again. Actually, that's not true. I saw him in my neighborhood the following week and he turned tail three hundred feet from me and ran away."

"Has there been anybody since?"

"Not even close. These have been lonely times for the pair of us."

"If you ignore the occasions I put you and our children in mortal danger, things weren't that bad when we were together."

"Apart from the near-death experiences, I loved the time I spent with you."

Alex looked deep into Sarah's eyes and held her hand. She smiled and squeezed his fingers.

"Would you be so kind as to accompany me to my hotel? Somehow, I don't want to be in this restaurant any more."

"You know something. We should go on vacation together and see how we get on. Meyer keeps telling me how Havana is a great party town if you have the gelt."

"One step at a time, Alex. Let's find out how we feel by the morning."

Alex grinned because Sarah was right. He might be a syndicate member again, but he was rushing ahead of himself. First, a night in Sarah's bed, then the next day they could plan the rest of their lives together.

THANK YOU FOR READING!

Get a free novella

Building a relationship with my readers is the very best thing about writing. I send weekly newsletters with details of new releases, special offers and other bits of news relating to my novels.

And if you sign up to the mailing list I'll send you a copy of the Alex Cohen prequel, The Broska Bruiser. Just go to www.leob.ws/signup and we'll take it from there.

Enjoy this book? You can make a difference

Reviews are the most powerful tools in my arsenal when it comes to getting attention for my books. Much as I'd like to, I don't have the financial muscle of a New York publisher. I can't take out full page ads or put posters on the subway. (Not yet, anyway).

But I do have something much more powerful and effective than that, and it's something that those publishers would kill to get their hands on.

A committed and loyal bunch of readers.

Honest reviews of my books help bring them to the attention of other readers.

If you've enjoyed this book I shall be very grateful if you would spend just five minutes leaving a review (it can be as short as you like) on the book's page. You can jump right to the page by clicking www.books2read.com/chiseler.

Thank you very much.

Leo

SNEAK PREVIEW

In Book 5, Cuban Heel…

"What I love about America is that the sidewalks are paved with gold."

"That's what I was told when I first arrived in New York, but the reality is different, Mr. President."

Alex Cohen and Meyer Lansky, two members of the organized crime elite, sat with Carlos Socarrás, the Cuban president as they sipped coffee and compared notes on the differences between their two great nations.

"I have seen the photographs, Alex—the walkways are so hot that the gold melts. I saw the steam, so it must be true."

Alex glanced at Meyer who maintained his fixed grin and stared at this excuse of a man before him.

"Maybe it's in Harlem. I didn't spend much time up there…"

The conversation continued in its stilted fashion for another five minutes before Meyer allowed it to slide away from the painful smalltalk and on to more important matters.

"I appreciate you are a very busy man, so I will get straight to it, if I may?"

A presidential nod indicated Socarrás was equally bored of pretending to care about the lives of the other people in his office.

"Cuba is a fabulous country but it is at a cusp of becoming a great nation."

"There is no need to flatter me, Meyer. The people of my country have been neglected for far too long. They are impoverished, tired and hungry. My hope is that I can find some ways to ease their lot during my time in office."

"And we think we can help you with that. I am not going to pretend that we can wave a magic wand and fix the difficulties you have here, but we do offer a route for a sustainable revenue stream in the long term with the opportunity to secure foreign investment now and in the future."

Socarrás leaned back in his velvety chair and mulled this thought around his head as he inhaled deeply on his cigar.

"Fine words, Meyer, but what is it that you are proposing?"

"I don't need to remind you that Havana is a short plane ride away from Florida, which means we have an opportunity to encourage Americans to fly over here and spend their hard-earned money."

"By any chance, do you have an idea as to what would attract those flies to travel to this midden?"

"Gambling. Alex and I created modern Las Vegas, which was nothing more than a desert town before we built casino-hotels and watched the money roll in."

Alex was surprised that Meyer had omitted the work done by Benny Siegel, the real creator of gaming Vegas, but the fella was in full sales pitch and not a historian.

"Mr. President, we can do same thing here. Build casinos and other sources of entertainment to attract American tourists to spend dollars in this country. And with your approval, we can do it."

Meyer sat back on the couch and gave Socarrás time to ponder the proposal. Alex couldn't tell if the guy was counting greenbacks in his mind or was concerned about the impact of foreign culture on this perfect isle.

"Foreign currency is always of interest to the President."

"Inward capital flows are healthy for a country."

"I was speaking personally, but what is good for the President is good for the people."

"The investors I represent would want to build a number of casinos over time. The model would be to replicate what we have already achieved in Vegas—only with less scrutiny of our day-to-day operations from the authorities."

"Meyer, I understand your situation. The American government has tried to shut down or curtail your business activities in Las Vegas several times and you want to be left in peace. You see Cuba as the place where you can make your money without hindrance."

"More or less, yes."

"But I still represent a government and the Cuban state needs to compensated for allowing you the freedom you seek."

"Mr. President, it goes without saying that we would want to pay our taxes and contribute to the fabric of this nation. All we ask in return is that we are not hampered by excessive regulation or undue scrutiny of what we do within the casinos themselves. We need to be left alone to make our money."

"Exactly so, I am sure you will have outgoings too and wish to have a level of privacy around the payments you make."

Meyer nodded and leaned forward, elbows resting on his knees.

"There is also the matter of how we show our appreciation to you for facilitating these arrangements."

"Half a million US dollars in small denominations, no consecutive serial numbers delivered to an address of my choosing before I lift a single finger to help you gentlemen destroy the moral fabric of my country."

To grab your copy, go to www.leob.ws/heel.

OTHER BOOKS BY THE AUTHOR

Alex Cohen

The Bowery Slugger (Book 1)
East Side Hustler (Book 2)
Midtown Huckster (Book 3)
Alex Cohen Books 1-3 (Due Late 2020)
Casino Chiseler (Book 4–Due Early 2021)
Cuban Heel (Book 5–Due 2021)
Hollywood Bilker (Book 6–Due 2021)
The Mensch (Book 7–Due 2021)
Alex Cohen Books 4-7 (Due 2022)

Stand Alone

The Case
The Death and Life of Penny Pitstop (erotic)
Awakenings (erotic, serialized)

The Lagotti Family

The Heist (Book 1)
The Getaway (Book 2)
Powder (Book 3)
Mama's Gone (Book 4)
The Lagotti Family Complete Collection (Books 1-4)

All books are available from www.leob.ws and all major eBook and
paperback sales platforms.

ABOUT THE AUTHOR

Leopold Borstinski is an independent author whose past careers have included financial journalism, business management of financial software companies, consulting and product sales and marketing, as well as teaching.

There is nothing he likes better so he does as much nothing as he possibly can. He has travelled extensively in Europe and the US and has visited Asia on several occasions. Leopold holds a Philosophy degree and tries not to drop it too often.

He lives near London and is married with one wife, one child and no pets.

Find out more at LeopoldBorstinski.com.